BLACK

JESUS

BLACK JESUS

JESUS

SIMONE FELICE

ALLEN&UNWIN

First published in 2011

The author wishes to thank To Hell With Publishing for their support.

Allen & Unwin
Sydney, Melbourne, Auckland, London

83 Alexander Street
Crows Nest NSW 2065
Australia
Phone: (61 2) 8425 0100
Fax: (61 2) 9906 2218
Email: info@allenandunwin.com
Web: www.allenandunwin.com

Cataloguing-in-Publication details are available
from the National Library of Australia
www.trove.nla.gov.au

ISBN 978 1 74237 725 4

Edited by Lucy Owen and Angus Cargill
Internal design by Lisa White
Typeset in 12.5/16 pt Sabon by Post Pre-press Group, Australia
Printed in Australia by Ligare Pty Ltd, Sydney

10 9 8 7 6 5 4 3 2 1

For Pearl and Jessie,
my better angels

PART
ONE

LIONEL WHITE

When Black Jesus came home from war a big pair of Stevie Wonder sunglasses hung on his face. Not because they made him look cool. That wasn't it. They gave him the glasses to hide the wreck the little plastic bomb had made of his eyes. He fought in Baghdad. He fought in Sadr City and out along the river and down all the bad roads in between. He fought in the Red Zone. He fought in the Green Zone. But most of all he fought the voice inside that whispered, *Boy, you don't belong.*

All through the night his fat mom Debbie drove south to the Marine Corps Air Station in her battered Chrysler wagon. Light rain on the roads. Memorial Day. After she signed her name on a clipboard and showed ID, they led her down the hall and into a room where a kid sat in a chair by the window, his seared head turned to face the glass where the cold sun he won't see again fell like a coin. That's when she came to him and touched his pale hair and said, 'Who did this to you?'

'Mom?'

'I'm right here.'

'I wanna go home.'

'I know you do, pumpkin. I know you do.'

Driving back up the New York State Thruway in the dark, one loose headlight dancing on the road before them, she tunes the radio awhile till she finds her station. Soft hits, yesterday's favorites. *Islands in the stream, that is what we are, no one in between, how could we be wrong, sail away with me to another world and we rely on each other, ah ha, from one lover to another, ah ha.*

She's doing 54 miles an hour. All the signs they pass say 65 since they raised the speed limit twenty years ago, but she doesn't care. Debbie's got her own way of doing things. Everybody howls past the Chrysler tonight. The radio's low and easy, and for the life of her she can't keep her eyes on the road because she can't keep her eyes off the boy right here in the musty seat beside her, so rigid and thin in his soldier's best. So young. So haunted and real.

Now they're passing Exit 17. Now she's got a hold
of his hand.

'Lot's changed since you been away, Lionel.'

He says nothing. Then he says, 'Like what?'

'Oh, I don't know.'

'Why'd you say it then?'

She looks at his face. Then she looks at the road.
After a while she says, 'There's a couple things I forgot to tell you on the phone.'

'Forgot?'

'Yeah.'

'Okay, so tell me now.'

'I burnt our house down.'

'What?'

'Our house.'

'It's a trailer, Ma.'

'Our home. I burnt our home down.'

'By accident?'

'Yes by accident.'

'I don't believe it,' he says, his dark glasses fixed
on her now.

'How come?'

''Cause I know you, Ma. You're a hustler. You're
a stone-cold pimp.'

'Lionel!'

'What?'

'Where'd you learn a thing like that?'

'I don't know. Over there. Guys.'

'What a thing to call your mother! That ain't the way I raised you, is it? Hearin' you talk like that makes me wanna shit in a bag and punch it.'

'Just tell me what happened.'

Unable to kill the little smile dawning at the corners of her mouth, the big woman breathes and glues her knee to the bottom of the steering wheel. She takes the window-crank with her free hand and twists the window down. She hasn't let go of his hand. She can't. And the cool night air cuts in.

'The Dairy Queen went belly up,' she tells him now above the hoarse wind.

'Whatta you mean?'

'Belly up. Shit the bed.'

'It closed down?'

'I'm afraid so.'

'But I—'

'Shhh. Don't be sad. I know how much you loved going there when you were a kid.'

'What's the DQ got to do with our place?' he says and pulls his hand away.

His mother breathes. After she breathes she says, 'Everything. It's got everything to do with us now, honey.'

He doesn't know what to say to that.

'Lionel? Earth to Lionel?'

'Don't call me that anymore.'

She looks at him with a screwed-up face and says, 'Whatta you mean? It's your name.'

'I'm Black Jesus now.'

'Excuse me?'

'Black Jesus. It's what they call me.'

'Who?'

'The guys in my squad.'

'Why?'

'I guess 'cause I'm so white. And 'cause my last name's White. And 'cause I was born on Christmas Day.'

'I don't get it.'

'One of the guys' dads was a Georgia preacher. Told him all kinds of crazy shit. Jesus married a hooker. Jesus was really a black man. Shit like that.'

'Nice.'

'It's called sarcasm, Ma. One time they had me stand on a oil barrel and hold my arms out like a scarecrow and—'

'They teased you?'

'They didn't mean nothin' by it. It was just their way of—'

A bird hits the windshield. The noise makes Lionel gasp and shake.

'What's that?' He needs to know, his fingers clamped tight to the corners of the seat now, his spine pressed against the imitation leather.

Debbie doesn't answer. Most of the bird went

careening off the glass, but not all. What looks like it might be part of the head remains. An eye. Black feathers and paper-thin bone like a Chinese fan. Blood running in a fine, bright rivulet down the windshield. She watches it run, off course like the picture she's tried to make of their life together. And as she follows its slant movements down to where the wipers lie sleeping, she thinks, *Lie to him, Debbie. Hasn't he tasted enough blood?*

Again he asks his mother what it was that made the sound.

'Nothing,' she says and pulls the handle for the wiper fluid and follows the bloodied wipers with her eyes, side to side as they whine and dance away the last of the bird.

It's grown cold in the Chrysler. The soldier shivers. Debbie rolls the window back up. In the distance she sees a car by the roadside with its hazards blinking red. She thinks of her toolbox in the trunk, her tire iron, her jack. Drawing near, she sees they've got the hood up. Thin smoke rising. Ten to one it's the radiator. Maybe she ought to stop and lend a hand. Not tonight. Tonight she's got to get her baby home.

Passing Exit 19, she draws a slow breath and says, 'Not everything burnt.'

He hears this and says, 'Like what?'

'Oh, I don't know. Like your Babar, for instance.'

The soldier keeps a poker face. Debbie turns her head to see how he's taken the news, a pirate's smile on her mouth.

A mile marker later he's asking, 'You went in after him?'

'Not exactly.'

'Firemen did?'

'Mmmmmmm, no.'

'Stop messin' with me, Ma.'

'I took him out the morning of.'

'Morning of what?'

'Day the house burnt up.'

'Trailer.'

'Home.'

'Not anymore.'

'Okay, I got him off your bed. Took a drive to the lake. Came back and the fire truck was in the driveway screamin' like a goddamn banshee. Neighbors gawkin'. Black smoke. Just like the movies. Stunk to high heaven but I couldn't help thinkin' it was kinda pretty, the smoke and fire and all.'

'Where's he now?'

'Babar?'

'Yeah.'

'Safe and sound.'

'Where at?'

'You'll see,' she says and pinches herself. *What a wicked thing to say.*

They drive the dark Thruway on until a sign for 'Exit 21: Catskill/Gay Paris/Cairo' looms loveless and plain in the headlights, an air of extraordinary permanence about its pose, like it wants you to think it's been here since before the trees. And you better believe it'll be leaning just the same when there's nobody left to ride these broken yellow lines home to nowhere.

She pays the toll lady with a fistful of nickels and two soft hits later they're idling hand in hand in the parking lot of the desperate everlasting summer afternoon she's dreamt up for them. Sad thing is nobody told her yesterday's not for sale. Not for a whole trailer full of insurance checks. Not for a thousand fishy kitchen fires. Yesterday's a dead bird. No calling it back.

Waddling around the hot hood with her boy's duffle bag over her shoulder, Debbie helps him from the car and takes him by the arm and leads him through the clean night air to the front door. Here they stand breathing. Wind in the trees. Nice moon. Silent, their poor little town. Smell of pine and garbage. They breathe and wait. One breath more. Then she touches the cool knob and turns it and draws him inside.

Inside smells strange. Like ten thousand days of onion rings and ketchup's stale ghost. Cleaning product. Watered-down Mountain Dew. Rainbow sprinkles. Dead freezer. Dead laughter. Faint smell of milk gone bad but perfect somehow, prehistoric and sweet in a desperate sense. In this heady air he sways, feels his mother move in the dark. Listens as the heel of her hand hits the lights. Hears the lights tremble on in this empty place, hoping maybe they'll reach him this time. No dice.

Debbie'd had some kind of little speech planned for just this moment. She wanted to tell him he was all that mattered to her. Nothing else. That come what may she'd be his shelter, his faithful one, his eyes if he'd let her. That this world is mean and she's sorry she brought him into it but she had to because of dreams she had when she was a girl. She'd wanted to tell him she never knew his father's name because she'd hushed the man when he tried to tell it in his hot car so that all the man would ever be was a voice and a smell and a heaviness in the dark. She'd had it in her head all this time the way she'd usher her boy home from the hell he'd lived, into the one place on earth she'd be sure he could smile. But the second she hit the switches and found him standing there in the hard light with that look on his face, all the ceremony fell out of her like a wet dead foal to the ground. So she keeps quiet. And suffers the sudden desert in her throat. And waits for him to open his mouth.

When he does, 'This is Dairy Queen,' he says.

'I did it for you.'

'We live here now?'

'Yeah. We live here now.'

'Just us?'

'Just us.'

Outside the wind sings high through the pines in the dark.

'Where's my bedroom?'

'Upstairs. In the garret.'

'The crow's nest?'

'You say tomahto, I say tomayto.'

'I always thought it was just for show.'

'Used to be.'

'I didn't think it was real.'

'It was real dirty. I scrubbed till my arm and hammer fell off. And I found you a bed. And I burnt sage.'

'What the hell's that?'

'Some freaky Indian mumbo jumbo Joe showed me.'

'Joe the Deputy?'

'It's leaves you burn.'

'Freakin' pyro.'

'It's to clean the space.'

'Clean it how?'

'I'm not sure. Bad spirits, I guess. His mom recommended it. Joe's part Mohican, you know. We been spending a little time together since the accident. He was the first one on the scene.'

'I bet he was.'

'Be nice.'

Debbie's smiling. It's been so long since they've talked this way. Feels good standing here in the quiet air. So many things to say. *Save it, Debbie. Don't ask about his eyes. Just tell him you'll help him upstairs.*

'Here, pumpkin. You gotta be whooped. Why don't we get you upstairs.'

'Black Jesus.'

'Whatever you say.'

She sits with him at the edge of the bed awhile and strokes his brow and pale hair.

'I said quit it, Ma.'

'I can't.'

The lamplight shows their faces, shows the shape of him under the blankets like somebody on a stretcher, his glasses undisturbed, Debbie in a sweater with geese on it.

'You sure you're warm enough?'

'I'm fine.'

'I can get another blanket if—'

'I'm fine.'

'Want Babar?'

'It's a stuffed elephant, Ma.'

'I know that. Do you want him?'

'No. Just leave him on the chair.'

His mother watches his mouth. It's older. It's changed. It screamed to her wretchedly half a world away in the loose blonde dirt of a town no one's heard of, in a country so old it moans a moan to answer the moan of the wind in the ruins. And now it's a blind man's mouth. A survivor's mouth. The old wonder gone from its contours. Wonder, the hardest thing to retrieve.

'Goodnight then.'

'Goodnight Ma.'

But she doesn't leave the great depression she's made in the mattress. Not just yet.

'I'm getting up now,' she says.

'Okay.'

'I mean it.'

The woman leans and gets to her feet. She breathes and reaches and kills the lamp. Then runs her fingers down the side of his thin bed, his cheap blanket in the dark. She lingers. Then she turns from him and walks to the ladder.

Now it's his turn. 'Mom?'

'What is it?'

'I saw someone.'

Debbie hangs with her hands clutching the first rung, her body lost in the space below. 'What's that mean?'

'I saw someone.'

'Where?'

'When they blew me up.'

Silence on the ladder. A hot pang straight through her. Hot in her sweater. All she can think to say is, 'Was he a friend?'

'It was a girl.'

Quiet on the ladder. Breathing.

'Like a woman,' he says.

'One of the locals?'

'No.'

'Then she musta been with the Marines. A nurse?'

'No. It was different.'

Debbie waits. Then says, 'What else did you see?'

In his bed in his very own dark he turns the question over like a card. 'Just her in the crazy sun,' he says. 'The dust and red sun and she was dancing. She was dancing.'

Debbie breathes. 'Black Jesus?'

'What?'

'Did the other boys see her?'

'I don't think so. I think just me.'

What do you say to that, Debbie? What the fuck do you say to that? 'Is she the last thing you saw?' Debbie hears herself ask.

'Yeah.'

'Well then try not to lose her.'

Quiet from the bed. Then, 'Okay, Ma. But I'm getting used to it.'

'Used to what?'

'Losing things,' he says, with a picture of the very pale blue eyes he had all his life staring back at him from their bathroom mirror one Christmas morning in his head.

Sometime in the night the soldier wakes and crawls from bed. Standing in the tiny room in his long johns, he leans on the balls of his feet and listens to his home. The trashy country quiet. The hum. An 18-wheeler out on the bypass and it's gone. Palms held out and groping now like maybe there'd be a piñata in the blackness that hides in its belly some other way his life could've turned out, had he been a more vigilant soul. But to hell with that piñata, because there are no what-could-have-beens, and vigilance means nothing to the grinning machinery of the world in its seedings and unmakings. And anyhow he's only looking for Babar. He will find him slumped in the folding chair by the wall and then he will carry him back to bed.

Black Jesus is a killer.

He was born in 1988.

He shakes.

Elephants never forget.

Black Jesus is shy, and a killer.

Black Jesus is white as a dove.

GLORIA

This freeway runs east. On and on until it touches the black and blue sky promising dawn out there in the flat beyond. A water tower in a field three miles distant. From here the girl can't tell what it is. Looks like a bell. Who's it ringing for? A little ways on and the water tower's plain to see. So how many tears will it hold? Her moped rattles beneath her like a robot pony in dreams. Her legs hurt. She took a painkiller at a pull-off just past the Arizona line. It hasn't done much. A tractor trailer blows past in a swaying riot of wheels and heat. She hums an old Madonna song inside her helmet. Her legs hurt like hell and the skyline's gone pink.

*

Three dollars and thirty-three cents. That's what the pump reads. Limping pitifully over the ground, she drags herself through the gas station door with the helmet still fastened to her head. In the back cooler she finds a Yoo-hoo and lifts the plastic shield from her face and drinks it down and screws the top back on and returns it to the cold rack, empty as her heart. Nobody saw.

At the counter she takes off her backpack and fishes a handful of one-dollar bills from the pocket in the front and lays them down. Tips from stripping. The man behind the counter has a little dog cradled up in his arm. It's white. So is his rodeo hat.

'Pump three?' he says.

The girl looks out through the doors to where her moped sits in the bright sun. 'I guess so. I'm the only one out there.'

'Three three three,' he says. 'Sounds kinda lucky to me.'

She counts the bills out and pushes the paper money across the counter one by one, all crumpled and raised like origami found in a madhouse cafeteria. Then the coins. The man straightens the dollars out and fingers the change into his palm and opens the register and sets them all in their place and shuts the drawer again. All of this done in a very deft and patient way, as if he'd spare any inconvenience his actions might have on the little dog nested there like a ceramic totem in the crook of his arm.

'How's that chopper on gas?' he says with a toss of his chin toward the pumps.

She looks back out at the moped she bought used from a movie extra for three hundred dollars on Valentine's Day, remembering the date because the extra had shared with her in confidence the tale of his liaison with a co-star and their plans for the night and their plans for a life together. She'd listened to the lie, the little keychain he'd given her turning clammy in her palm under the parking lot lights, and she felt sad and thought to herself, *It's all right, lonesome dove, you can have a talking part in my B-movie tonight and I'm gonna love your crappy moped better than anyone in this whole shameless city could hope to love anything.*

'Gas?' she says, and she's queasy, a dizzying pain that strikes at her core.

'Yeah. What kinda mileage you gettin'?'

'It's funny,' she says, 'I never thought to do the math.'

'Nothin' funny 'bout gasoline, dolly. That stuff's the devil's dick-wash.'

The girl smiles the best she can. 'What's that supposed to mean?'

'I'm not sure. Just like the sound of it.'

'Hey, can you recommend me a scenic route?' she says. 'I need to get off the interstate.'

'Where you headed?'

'Away from Los Angeles.'

'Can't blame ya,' he says and fondles the dog's head. 'Scenic route. Hmmm. Let's see. I believe I can do ya one better.'

He turns around and hunts through a stack of old vacation maps in a wire stand on the wall. While he's got his back to her she steals a lighter from a display by the register. The lighter says 'Never Forget' above a cheap likeness of the Twin Towers.

'Here we go,' says the man turning around and laying on the counter a faded state map boasting a cactus wren on the cover. 'This'll git ya off the beaten path, sure as shit.'

'I don't really have any money to—'

'Stop right there, doll. This here's gratis. From one outlaw to another.'

'Thanks,' she says. 'You're sweet.' The lighter in her pocket just got a little heavier. 'I better hit the road,' she says and her hand is shaking.

She swats the helmet's pink shield down over her face and raises a hand in farewell and goes limping to the door.

Almost there when the man says, 'What happened to your legs you don't mind me askin'?'

A few more steps and she's leaning on the door

and her slight weight cracks it and a dose of clean desert air hits her. She lifts the shield from her face one more time and breathes.

'Last night the guy I live with hit them with an aluminum bat till I passed out on the carpet. He did that 'cause I got into the City Ballet Company,' she says. 'They just loved my audition. You should have seen me.'

'Fuck's sake,' whispers the man.

With a nod of her helmet the girl motions to her right leg. 'I think I heard this one crack. Like a stick on the beach. He said, "I'm going to kill you." Then he said, "I love you." Then he laughed like a hyena and took his pants off. When I woke up he was asleep and I split. Put some things in this bag and rode all night. Have you ever seen a million pale windmills all turning in the dark?'

The man shuts his eyes a moment. As if he'd find them turning there. But all he finds is blackness. And a type of despair he hadn't counted on today. 'You look after yourself,' he calls through the empty store but she's already out on the pavement in the sun, dragging herself to the pumps. A trucker passes her on his way in to pay for diesel and the trucker squints and looks her up and down.

'People,' says the man to his white little dog. 'When the hell they ever gonna learn?'

*

21

Sky of red. Dusk on this quiet road off Highway 180. Clocking no more than 25, she hugs the white line at the shoulder. Signs that say 'Petrified Forest National Park' come on and recede. Souvenir shop. Sky of rusty blue violence. Cold desert night drawing closer by the mile, sharp at her fingers and neck. Memory. Throttle. Voices in her helmet. Smell of burnt brakes on a hill. Sky of burnt sapphire.

Through the pink plastic she spies a huddled shape in the road ahead. Something hit by somebody's car, somebody's truck. The girl slows the scooter and brakes it to a stop and plants her feet and looks down at the body. It's a bear. A small one. A young one. And it's still alive.

The runaway shivers and turns her head back the way she came and looks that long stretch over to be sure no one is upon her. No one is. Returning to the mess at her feet, she finds it lying on its side in its own hot viscera with its arms sort of crossed at its heart and its knees drawn up and something about this pose disarms the girl and she starts to cry.

'You poor thing,' she says and lifts the shield and the tears are hot down her face. The animal's chest rises slow, falls slow and its eyes are wet in the scooter's lamplight and very beautiful and she's not sure but she thinks they're looking back into hers.

The bear's brunette coat is slick with blood as she drags it onto the loose roadside gravel. White-hot pain through her legs up into her mind. In the gathering darkness she sits by its side and strokes the crown of its head, both of them broken and strange.

'It's okay,' she tells it. 'You can go now.' The animal blinks and shudders. 'You can go. It's okay, there's gotta be a better place than this.'

LIONEL WHITE

In Gay Paris, New York, there's an Arab gas station and a few churches and a small brick post office and three or four gargantuan country boarding houses falling into varied stages of disrepair, tall weeds, paint peeling, bungalows in back, screen doors sliced or gone, leaning relics of a different time, lost American summer. There's the Dairy Queen you already know about and the old folks' home and a coke house down the street to which everyone turns a blind eye. There's a bar & grill called Shakespeare's at the traffic light, a firehouse, a worn metal sign that says 'Welcome To Gay Paris, Stay A While' and little else.

When Lionel White was a kid he was very frail and quiet and one summer they built a giant billboard of the Marlboro Man on horseback with a six-shooter in the empty lot next to Shakespeare's in the middle of town. Everybody hated it, called it an eyesore. But whoever put it up knew that a million city people in cars would pass it on their way to the lake and ski lifts and Hasidic summer retreats and Korean Christian camps ten miles up the mountain road. Everybody passes through, maybe stop for gas, stop for ice cream, maybe change a flat tire. Not many reasons to stay.

So one summer the Marlboro Man took up camp and towered arrogant and bizarre above all Gay Parisians and the kids hit him with rocks and their folks shook their heads and cursed him, but they all figured there was nothing they could do about it.

All but one man. A legend, God rest his soul. An ex-long-haul-trucker-turned-minister known simply as Interstate. Interstate who liked to drink and had a tough wiry frame and cold blue eyes that lit up his old face. He wore cowboy boots and listened to Dolly Parton and Styx on a boom box from the porch of the camper he lived in next to the gas station. And that year, one night late in August, he left his boom box playing and walked down the highway in pajamas with a hunting rifle and shot the Marlboro Man all to hell. And when Joe the Deputy showed up and had to put the cuffs on him, he smiled at Interstate and asked him why he did it and Interstate smiled back and said, 'That big fucker drew first.'

He spent the night in county jail and got away with a fine and never paid it, and after a while they tore the holey billboard down and life went on like before. Some kids found a piece of the giant cowboy's hat in the weeds behind the lot and they brought it to Shakespeare's and Mona swapped them for Cokes and hung it on the wall by the jukebox with a little silver plaque that read 'Don't Fuck With Interstate'.

And in the very early mornings you'd see him smoking on his porch watching the colors in the sky with Dolly singing from the speakers on the rail and he'd minister when the money was good and last year he got lung cancer and didn't do the chemo like they told him and died on his birthday, Halloween.

If you've ever been through town it would've been hard to miss the trailer Lionel grew up in. A little ways past the gas station you'd have seen it standing tan and cockeyed in the last mangy yard before the mountain road rises hard and twists its way up through state land along the rushing creek.

And there by the trailer, under blue tarps and various makeshift canopies thrown up throughout the years, you'd have found Fat Debbie's perpetual yard sale, ever-shifting bric-a-brac on wobbly tables or simply on the ground, dangling from hooks and hangers, perched on stands, in baskets with masking-tape price tags stuck on each treasure, marked in her own surprisingly fine hand, to aid the frugal shopper on his way through a maze of generally worthless things. Never tell her that, she'll smack your face. In Deb's mind her yard sale offers all the same mystery and charm as, say, some silk and spice bazaar in the Holy Land might've once, some bustling marketplace in the furthest Orient. Just instead of a monkey and myrrh and an abacus, she's got a stuffed cat and Right Guard for Men and a calculator she stole from Wal-Mart. The yard sale is her life's work, her opus. And on any given day, winter, spring, summer or fall, you could've stopped and gotten out and approached to the sound of soft hits on the radio and she'd probably have tried to sell you a pair of ratty moon boots, a TV, a mirror, a set of Russian dolls just missing one, a sea chest, a painting of a wolf, a motorcycle helmet, an ash-tray she'll swear belonged to FDR, a painting of an Indian on horseback, a ski jacket, a knife set, Candy Land in a box missing just a few cards, an evening gown, a Crockpot, a turquoise anklet, a sugar bowl, a bikini top, a painting of Jerusalem at twilight, a lamp, an Atari, a fish tank, Ghostbusters on VHS.

Lionel's been home now for two weeks and if it ever crossed his mind that moving to Dairy Queen would have somehow put an end to his mother's bazaar he was sorely mistaken. She's a crafty one, that Debbie, a sort of Boss Tweed in pink sweatpants and dirty white Reeboks. Since the move she's been working with renewed zeal, driving around the back roads, stopping at the odd house to ask the guy in the driveway if there's anything in his garage he wants to get rid of, maybe a camera, maybe a rocking horse? With the help of her new flame called Joe, she's put up better tarps than ever against the rain, and together they've spray-painted a big wooden sign that says 'Flea Market. Donations Welcome. Lighten Your Load. One Man's Junk is Another's Delight!' and hung it where the Dairy Queen logo used to swing.

Since he's been home the rain's let up. There are birds singing and the lilacs that line the road are in late bloom, but he can't see them. He's sad. He's quiet and sad.

Debbie calls to him up the ladder. 'Lionel?'

He doesn't answer.

She tries again. 'Black Jesus?'

'What?'

'Come outside, it's a sunny day.'

'Why?'

''Cause I got you something.'

'What?'

'Come down and you'll see,' she says, and then quietly to herself, 'What's wrong with you, Debbie? You really gotta stop doing that.'

She hears him shuffling around, his footsteps in the attic, and she goes to the top of the ladder and tries to take his hand but he pulls it away and says, 'I can do it. Stop treating me like a baby.'

'I just wanna make sure you—'

'I'm a Marine, Mom,' he says and his voice is strange.

'Okay, babe. You're right. I'm sorry,' she says. 'I'll be outside, business is pickin' up, sold a Dictaphone this morning.'

'Dick what?'

'Don't be fresh.'

In a little while he appears at the top of the ladder in grey jogging pants and makes his way down slowly, rung by rung. Last night he dreamt of the war he was in.

He watched a child die in the street. Its mother came running, an emerald green scarf trailing behind her in the hot wind. There was shooting from a window, and the smell of cooking spice, and a loud siren and men shouting in his own language and a language he doesn't know.

He cowered in a tight doorway. Then he felt the blast and stepped from where he hid, and as he came into the street glass from the windows above rained down on his helmet and cut his hands. When the shooting stopped he knew the sniper was dead. He turned back to where he'd seen the child cut down and a small crowd had gathered there. He started towards them and as he did the woman in the green scarf got to her feet with the little body cradled up in her arms, its brown head limp as a bell.

'Go home!' she shouted at him in the Queen's English, her face calm and pretty. 'Please, just go home!'

Now here he is, crossing the room with his black glasses and his hands out in front of him, feeling his way through the maze of boxes and clothing racks, the picture frames leaning, past a broken guitar, a mannequin, a bicycle tire, groping in the dark to find the door that'll take him out into the parking lot where his mom is waiting. And when she sees him there she stops fidgeting with a set of painted teacups and comes to him and takes his hand. This time he lets her and she leads him down the steps and out into the heart of her flea market where a wicker rocking chair seesaws slightly in the summer wind.

'Have a seat, Your Highness,' says Debbie to the boy.

'What am I sittin' on?'

She takes his hand and sets it on the arm of the rocker. 'It's old but it'll give you an excuse to hang out with me.'

'Just what I always wanted,' he bullshits and eases himself down into the chair, the muscles in his forearms quivering as he grips the wood.

'Go for it,' he hears his mother say.

'Go for what?'

'Rock. It'll be good for your head.'

'What's wrong with my head?'

'Nothing's wrong. I just want you to be happy.'

'Good luck,' he says. 'Where's my painkillers?'

'You're all out.'

'Fucker.'

'I'll go to Catskill and get more. Rite-Aids or CVS?'

'I don't care, just get them.'

'Okay, honey. I'll be right back.'

Once she's gone he starts to rock. The wicker on his spine. Gas truck goes by. The dull ache in his temples, something he's learnt to wear, crown of thorns—what would he be without it?

GLORIA

In the diner they watch her come up the steps and open the door, the waitress and a handful of vague men at breakfast. They'd get up and help her but they're not sure she's real. It's just before the sun, that hour when the new day's meaning is still unclear, when life is something like theatre and who it is you're meant to play can swing like a hinge.

As if she's carried some dire news for them all to hear, the girl stands in her helmet swaying on the tan linoleum like a refugee from space, all pigeon-toed and warped at the knees with grinning bunnies and baskets and all the colored pomp of Easter hanging from strings overhead spinning drunkenly in the wind she's let in.

'You all right, doll?' says the waitress, her painted-on eyebrows raised and her hand frozen in the cash drawer.

The doll doesn't answer. She just starts to fall. Like a gutted building after dynamite. Quick jumps a man from the counter with a howling cayote on his t-shirt. Moving like a wrestler he takes the girl up in his arms before she can hit the ground and carries her limp figure to the door. The waitress puts her hands on her hips. The diners watch in dull amazement, forks frozen in mid-bite.

'Where you goin' with her?' says one.

'Don't worry,' says the man with the cayote on his shirt. 'She's with me.'

'What about yer eggs?' barks the waitress.

'Put it on my tab,' he says and they're gone.

When she comes to, she's in his truck and there's a beat-up dreamcatcher on the mirror and a horse-shoe on the dash and they're making their way down a dirt road with pines out the shaky window. Pain and nausea flood the girl and new daylight floods the cab where dead coffee cups and apple cores litter the floor sweet with rot.

'Keep your leg still.'

'Where are you taking me?'

'Up the road.'

'Where?'

'Where nobody can find you. Isn't that what you're lookin' for?'

The girl's head spins. 'Where's my moped?' she says.

'It's in the back. You're gonna need it once we get you fixed up.'

'You're helping me?'

'Yes.'

'Why?'

'I know what a beat-up girl looks like. It's what my mother was, her eyes always frozen like a question with nobody to answer it. Growing up, I seen enough shit to know who's runnin', enough huntin' to know quarry when I see it.'

'Quarry?'

'Somebody's after you, right?'

She's fainting again. She breathes and says, 'I don't know, he might be.'

The truck rumbles along and the driver has both hands on the wheel and his back is straight and his pilot's sunglasses scan the road for ruts and deer and dogs. In her head the girl feels afraid, but in her body she does not. She's finding out that safety is a word that means different things as life unfolds. There's shelter, and there's shelter. There's a dry dead rabbit at the edge of the road and tiny wildflowers at the edge of the trees and her eyes frozen like a question see double and the tape deck sings a song she used to dance to.

In the club she grinds the pole and a dark orange light throbs above her. Men watch from round tables and an old hit called 'Gloria' blasts from a speaker hung from the ceiling by chains. She has small tits for a stripper. Gloria, Gloria. She has long legs and her mouth is painted and one man leans to another's ear with a boast and they laugh and crash their glasses together in the air-conditioned riot of want and noise. Gloria. The girl lunges down and plants her palms on the floor and points her ass in the air and works it from side to side.

When next she opens her eyes she's lying on her back in a small bed in a plain clean room. There's a glass of water on a little stand by her side and she sits up and takes a drink. The water feels good in her dry mouth. As she puts the glass down she's aware of a change in the way things feel below her waist. With her fingers she peels away a light blanket to find her right leg propped up on pillows and set in a sort of splint, a cool thin length of metal under her knee, clean bandages wrapped up tight.

Through a sliding glass door on the other side of the room the girl can see a dry lawn and thin white clouds in a big sky. Then a man comes into the picture. He's holding a short rope and leading a horse towards the house. As they come closer, she can tell the horse is hurt, it hangs it head, it staggers in a slow approach. The man bends to the animal's ear and tells it things, he kisses its face, he strokes the top of its head.

When they get to the sliding glass door he opens it and, to the girl's surprise, walks the animal right into the room.

'This is Cher,' he says with a toss of his chin toward the horse.

'Hi Cher,' she says from the bed, still dazed.

'I'd complete the introduction but I don't know your name.'

'Gloria,' she hears herself say.

'Just Gloria?'

'Yes.'

'Good, then we got two divas on the property. Cher meet Gloria.'

A light rain's begun to fall outside and the man reaches and pulls the glass door closed. Cher lifts her head and makes a soft noise with her nose. The runaway smiles and feels warm in her blanket and knows she's safe here.

'Who are you?' she says to him.

'Charles P. Shoemaker the fourth, last in a long line of weirdoes.'

'You fix shoes?'

'Good guess. I fix horses. Try 'n' fix 'em, I suppose is a better way to say it.'

She looks at him, reaches for the glass and takes a drink. 'You ever fix a broken chick before?'

'Nope. Shoulda fixed my ex-wife, the tramp. Tied her tubes up like a balloon giraffe.'

The girl laughs and takes another drink of water and sets the glass back down. 'Well, there's a first time for everything,' she says.

'Yeah, that's what they say.'

After a moment she says, 'Thank you, Charles.'

'Chuck.'

'Thank you, Chuck—for helping me. I'm really all alone out here.'

'No family?'

'None that I care about.'

'A beau?'

'What?'

'A boyfriend.'

'He's who did this to me.'

Chuck doesn't know what to say to that.

'He's a critic for the LA Times,' she says softly, her mind going hazy again. 'I think he loves me. He just didn't like it 'cause I'm a rising star in the City Ballet and I—'

'Shhh,' says the man. 'You just rest. You're gonna need some real convalescing.'

'Fancy word,' she says through a broken smile.

'I'm a fancy guy,' he says and spits into the sink on the wall for effect. 'You got a cracked tibia.

You're gonna need to keep your leg elevated and get some rest. You can stay here till you're better. Then you can climb on that ridiculous scooter of yours and sail the seven seas to your heart's content. Just don't be a goddamn daredevil.'

Days spent slowly walking the grounds on the crutches he gave her, out to the edge of the farm where an electric fence-line runs, horses in, wolves out. These jagged mountains in panorama, each breath of high desert air a weird miracle in her lungs. Charles P. comes and goes like a shadow. She sees him in the distance, hears his truck in the driveway, watches him pass by a window, or out in the field, they'll share a smile, a wave, a passing word.

One afternoon she sits at the base of a big lonely tree, a ways from the house, her back against its trunk, her eyes shut against the bright sun on her face. A very pregnant mare makes its silent approach and now stands by and lowers its white head and touches its mouth to the stripper's brow.

'Huh,' she breathes, halfway lost in her sun-dazed head, opening her eyes to find the animal towering above.

Reaching her hand up to meet the mare, the girl sets to lightly stroking the crown of its head, the tight coarse hair above its big dark eyes.

'Where'd you come from?' she asks and the horse shoots a breath of warm air from its wet nose, glad of her touch. 'I guess you should be wondering the same thing about me,' she says, still soothing its head, and looks past the white mare to some far-away point on the horizon. 'I was born on the coast of Maine, but somehow ended up in Venice Beach, sea to shining sea. My real name's Desiree, my stage name is Desire, and now I guess I'm Gloria. What's the difference anyway? This world will drink a girl dry and piss you out and never even ask your name.'

Next night she wakes from a dream and gets dressed in the dark. She sits at the edge of the bed and stares out the glass door, her breath the only sound.

Shouldering her backpack she gets to her feet and works the aluminum crutch into her armpit. She makes for the door, parts the sliding glass and hobbles through the yard in silence towards the shed where her little black steed awaits. Now she's got her helmet on. Now she turns the key.

In her dream she walked along a rushing stream in a quiet wood, her naked feet landing easy on the moss and kicking up last year's leaves as she went. Smell of pine. Sun through the trees. Then by and by she came upon a girl no more than ten sitting on a rock at the water's edge, dangling her toes in the current. The dreamer smiled to see such a quaint sight. Just like a postcard. But when the child turned to her and their eyes met, her smile turned to cancer because she knew the little face as her own, knew the purple barrettes and how sad and fucked-up the passing of time is, knew the halting voice that asked just one thing as she woke, 'How could you let this happen to us?'

LIONEL WHITE

Late in the afternoon, Joe the Deputy pulls his white and red Ford into the Dairy Queen parking lot, whistling along to a Pink Floyd song on the radio. He checks his hair in the rear-view mirror and fixes his greasy part and opens the squad car door with a shoebox in his hand and heads for the maze of tables under the blue tarps where he knows his big hot siren awaits.

Joe's spent his whole life in Gay Paris. His father was a full-blooded Mohawk who made his living playing a wild Indian at the Carson City Western theme park down on Route 32. There he shot arrows and led the rain dance and threw tomahawks into trees and rode a sad horse bareback and drank himself to sleep in the dark when the gates were locked.

When business dried up and the place closed down, it's said the old diabetic left his insulin in the refrigerator of his camper one night and walked into the woods and never came out. A half-hearted search party gave it a week before they ruled him dead. And to this day Joe's old mother Bea swears his father comes to her as a hawk at the window of her little room in the nursing home up the road, Serenity Grove. And with the home shopping network blasting on the TV and a black feather in her pale braid and a cup of Earl Grey in her thin, bony hand she'll tell her son the hawk came with secrets last night, news from the other side, a message from Auntie Arleen, a warning from so-and-so, don't work the night shift next week, Joe Boy, something will happen, don't drive past the coke house so slow, they've got your number, and so on. And though he loves her like crazy, the Deputy has never taken much stock in the old lady's voodoo. He grinds his teeth when she talks this way and his high brown cheekbones tell the story of his heart: *Man, I wish I could believe in this shit, maybe if I did I wouldn't be fifty-six years old and so alone.*

But all that changed the morning he came upon Debbie's burning trailer and she pulled him into the bushes and whispered in his ear and gave him a weird handjob to the crackling of vinyl and particle board so he'd not call the fire truck just yet and so he'd hide the gas can she used to light the fire in the trunk of his car and never tell.

Now here he is, ducking his head under the tarp to find her blind son teetering slowly in his creaky rocker back and forth beside a small chest of drawers with ceramic frogs on top. The cop takes off his hat and says, 'Hi Black Jesus.'

'Hi Joe.'

'Brought you a present, man.'

'Why?'

'I don't know, figur'd it'd cheer you up. It's nothin' really, just somethin' I had when I's a kid. Found it in the closet and thought you might like it.'

Joe squats down before the rocker and puts the shoebox in the soldier's hand. Lionel takes it and sets it on his lap and starts to lift the top but stops as he hears his mom kick open the screen door she hung in the DQ entry. She strides out with lipstick on her mouth and a violet ribbon in her dirty-blonde hair.

Her uniformed stud looks her up and down and says, 'Well, look at you.'

'Ditto. Whatchu bring my baby?'

'I was in the process of finding out,' huffs Lionel, 'till you two honeymooners got goin'.'

'Well, open it,' she says.

'Yeah,' says Joe. 'Open it.'

The blind boy takes the top of the shoebox in both hands and lifts it and drops it on the gravel.

Then he reaches in and feels the worn wooden handle, follows it up till it turns to metal, smells the metal, smells the age, feels the cool sharp head.

'An axe?'

'Close,' says Joe. 'It's a tomahawk.'

'What's he gonna do with that?' says Debbie.

'I thought I'd teach him to throw it.'

'Throw it at what?'

'Trees.'

'How the hell's he—'

'Mom,' Lionel breaks in.

'Yes, honey?'

'I like it. Thanks, Joe.'

'It just looks dangerous,' she raves. 'You know he's on painkillers. Plus I bet you anything we could get thirty bucks for it if we put a tag on it. At least thirty, it's a antique, maybe even—'

'Mom!'

'Yes, honey?'

'It ain't for sale.'

As he speaks, a hybrid rent-a-car pulls up and two good-looking men step out and approach the country bazaar.

Joe eyes them and whispers, 'Check out these two homos.'

'I don't give a rat's ass if they're eff-in' Jihadis so long as they buy somethin',' snaps Debbie in a whisper and Joe shuts his trap.

'Can we help you?' she calls to them in her sweetest voice.

The taller one answers in an English accent, something as remote to Gay Paris, New York, as a white tiger, 'We saw the sign for the flea market.'

'Indeed you did. I assure you gentlemen we got somethin' for everybody.'

'Yeah, I think I saw a butt plug in the bin,' whispers Joe and Black Jesus chuckles, his hands on the hatchet.

'Lovely,' says the tall one in leather pants who's picked up a cold war era globe and begun to spin it round.

'In London we call this sort of thing a car boot sale.'

'That's a globe,' say Debbie.

'No, this,' he makes a sweeping gesture with his hand. 'When people try to sell their junk.'

'That's cute,' smiles Debbie. 'But as you can see, we've got a whole hell of a lot more than boots to offer. Generally we say garage sale. Or yard sale. But we figur'd flea market had a more worldly ring to it.'

'A little classier,' adds Joe.

'Yeah,' says Black Jesus.

The Englishmen look down at the strange soul in the rocking chair, his dark shades, his stoned grimace, his sweatpants, his army boots untied and his big thumb petting the hatchet blade.

'No arguing with that,' says the tall one and sets the globe back on the table.

'I think it's time to go, Roger,' says the other.

GLORIA

If the map of her country were a paint-by-numbers kit she bought to distract herself from pain, the battered square that is Missouri would be halfway colored in with a dull metallic gray because she would have dropped her paintbrush on the table in disgust by now and gone upstairs to bed.

It's been raining since yesterday and she's holed up in an all-night gas station/restaurant, sitting in a faded red booth with her knapsack in her lap and her head against the window. Outside, a man tries his credit card at the pump and is denied. He takes the card out and looks at it and tries again but is twice denied. He kicks the pump. He spits. He curses it and gets back in his truck and drives out into the rain. Strange, but everything beyond the window takes place in the most provocative silence, every horn blast, every semi roaring by. Even the wind. Even the pouring rain. Knives scrape plates and glasses clink and sometimes the people in the place exchange words in a language that's become remote to her somehow, though it's the only one she knows. The big clock by the door says 6:49 and she can hear it tick as her broken heart keeps its own funny time. She thinks of a day long ago when her mom picked her up outside 4th grade in their rusty little escort and instead of driving home they found the highway and spanned the entire state of Maine before she fell asleep to the radio and the hum of wheels, the hiss of the motor. All to escape her bad dad. Some things never change.

Next morning she woke in the passenger seat and her mom was still out cold, the faded Madonna t-shirt she wore catching the morning light, her nipples showing through, her teeth grinding to a dream it would take the girl another ten years to understand. She opened the door very quietly and stepped out into the parking lot they'd spent the night in. It was cold at that hour. And there was only one other car, some old red thing with a square of cardboard in the windshield that read '$850 or Best Offer'.

They were on a quiet highway she'd never seen.

A garage in the distance, a white trailer across the road and woods all around. When she spun herself back towards the trees they'd parked under her eyes met a big wooden sign: 'Mystery Spot'.

Time and weather had worked at the paint but she could still read it easy. And what a thing to behold when you're nine. Before life on man's earth has siphoned all the fine mystery away like so much gas from a chainsaw. And walking towards it, the girl felt hot inside and drawn to it somehow. Mystery Spot. And coming close she found a tin box that said 'Take One' and there were pamphlets inside and she took one and folded it into the back pocket of her jeans and then she heard her mom yell, 'Get back in the car—it's time to go.'

Now Gloria looks into her cold coffee. Now she closes her eyes and breathes slowly and opens them back up and unzips her pack and rummages inside and pulls out a brittle paper and lays it on the table. Mystery Spot.

With the rain streaming sideways down the window and a man coughing in the booth behind her and the painkiller she took not helping her leg at all, she sits in this depressed waystation and opens the pamphlet, this relic of her past she's carried with her through all the moves, all the tears and changes:

Deep in the heart of the Catskills
you'll find a place so strange and wondrous,
where an unexplained phenomenon of gravity
has spawned a hair-raising attraction
for the whole family to enjoy.

COME TO THE MYSTERY SPOT,
where water runs uphill, chairs dance on
their own and things are not what they seem.

Located on Route 32, close to the NY State Thruway,
just north of Carson City, a stone's throw from
where Rip Van Winkle had his long snooze.

ADULTS $5/CHILDREN AND SENIORS $2.50

Take a chance and visit the Mystery Spot,
where just about anything can happen.

LIONEL WHITE

A phone rings in the lobby of the Tigris Hotel but the man at the desk can't answer it because he's dead. The plastic flowers by his hand are just as still as he is and PFC Lionel White is in the stairwell, his black machine gun crossed at his chest, his back to the plaster wall.

That goddamn phone.

A paranoid silence coats the second floor like spray paint. Even the dust mites in the sliver of light above the boy's helmet linger and wait in the drum-tight air.

And that terrible phone.

Then gunshots and wholesale mayhem on the landing, six steps up. All hell loose in Room 213. All in a day's work. But our Marine is heading downstairs, somebody's gotta answer that phone.

That it's his own voice waiting at the other end of the line is a thing made no less chilling by the simple fact that this is only a dream. Just another square in the quilt of hurt and color and stink that's been stitching itself nightly in his attic room since first he came home from that desert. Babar in his bed.

'Hello.'

'Hi Lionel.'

'Who's this?'

'You know who it is.'

'Why are you calling me? There's people dying upstairs.'

'I'm afraid.'

'Afraid of what?'

'I don't know.'

'Say it, pussy!'

'I can't.'

'Say it!'

'I'm afraid of what's gonna happen to you.'

Silence on the phone line. Hard shouts and machine-gun fire in the heat and wreck upstairs. Stillness in this tacky lobby. Dead man still dead. His cheek against the desktop, his arms spread wide. Little black fly on his brown hand. Today's the dead man's daughter's fifth birthday. She was born the night this city fell. She wants a Cinderella DVD. God, would she die for that long yellow hair.

54

'Did you hear what I said?'

'Yeah, you're afraid. What else is new?'

'I'm afraid of what's coming.'

'What, you got a friggin' crystal ball?'

'No, but I see things.'

'What's that mean?'

'I know what they did to that girl.'

'What girl?'

'You know just what I mean. You weren't supposed to be there. You watched them nail her up. You watched them do what they did.'

'Stop. Please.'

'And how she glistened with gas. It's been eating you up. It's made you close right up to everyone. Especially yourself. That means you and me.'

'Now I know you're certifiably bat-shit.'

'I just don't wanna see you rock the rest of our life away a sad pill junky in that chair.'

'What chair?'

'The one at Mom's yard sale.'

'How the hell could that happen? I'm a Marine. I'm a motherfuckin' Marine.'

Now the voice on the phone is quiet. And the shooting upstairs sounds like firecrackers in a oil barrel at midsummer, Anytown, USA. And the dead man's eyes are open. And glassy. And a chill shoots through the soldier in this hot lobby, his long black gun on the desk, the silent receiver against his dusty ear.

'Hello,' he says. 'Where'd you go?'
No one at the other end. Silence.
'Is this a joke? Please say something.'
Nobody. Little black fly on Lionel's arm now.
Little black fly on his face. And upstairs they keep
shooting. Upstairs and all around the world.

GLORIA

The rain's stopped falling and everything feels a
little cleaner as she motors along and the passing
countryside spools out before her like a roll of Wal-
Mart film she hid away in a drawer somewhere. In
five days' time she's covered three and a half states,
seen a lady with elephantiasis in a van at a gas station, experienced a surprise orgasm brought on by
the incessant hum of the moped seat between her
legs, nothing to write home about. She found a
suede purse in a truck-stop bathroom, pocketed the
cash and went to mail the purse to the address on
the woman's driver's license, but as she copied the
street name and zip code on the package her eyes
strayed to the face in the picture ID and the face
seemed so dreadfully used up that she cursed herself

for being such a klepto and put the money back and mailed the thing off and cried inside her pink helmet for miles down the road.

Maybe I won't dance again. Hard to think of a time when I didn't have this pain. Weird how fast we forget the way things used to be. Guess it's good though. Guess it's built into us somehow, this way of forgetting, helps us deal with the holes left in us when things we love get taken away. I was so close to it. So close to dancing for real. The ballet. Listen to the sound of that. What could be better? The ballet. Like a bird at your window. No, like a room of colored glass where you go when you're high on songs. Just when I could close my eyes and do it. Just when I could see the quiet crowd waiting. Just when I could smell my own sweat on the stage, that's when he took it away from me. The ballet. It was okay when I stripped. He was fine with that. First I thought it was the money I brought home from the club. That if I quit The Cat House to really do my dream he'd have to pay all the bills. But it wasn't the money. He made plenty. Ross Klein. The big critic. Big deal. My last boyfriend was a biker, he was tough and greasy and out of work but boy was he a teddy bear, wouldn't hurt a fly, and looking back I think he might have really loved me.

Then this one. Ross Klein with his silver laptop. Ross Klein with his father's boat. His place in

Venice. His hairdo. His blog. All he ever wanted to do was write songs. That was his dream. That's what he told me once when we were drunk. That maybe he could write one good enough to fix his fucked-up heart, one good enough to bring his mom back. Sad, but it took him thirty years to realize he wasn't any good at it. So where do you turn after that? Guess if he couldn't write the songs to make the young girls cry he figured he'd just pick apart other people's in a newspaper.

So when I told him I finally got the audition it was too much for him I think. The bat he hit me with still had the price tag on it. My girl Brown Shugah at The Cat House told me something once, 'It's the perfect white boys you gotta watch out for. You can tell by the way they look into their own eyes in the mirror. They got their cake from day one and when they can't eat it too they snap. And when they snap it's like Nightmare On Elm Street.' Guess I shoulda listened to her.

At a gravel pull-off a little ways past a thin metal sign that said 'Effingham, Illinois' she shuts her engine down and kicks the kickstand out and takes her helmet off and hangs it on the handlebars. Struggling past a group of picture-takers, she makes her way through the chain-link fence and limps past the edge of the gravel into a field of green corn that reaches out in all directions to touch a vague horizon. Gloria didn't bother to read the big silver plaque by where she parked. The one that boasted 'America's Biggest Crucifix', but she can see the thing for herself right there in the field. What a monster. All white and shining in the sun. Rising up from the quiet earth like an eerie daydream. Something sudden. Something altogether warped.

Now the pilgrims at the roadside in pastel-colored clothes who've driven a hundred miles to this holy place lay their cameras by and watch her.

'What's she doin' out there?'

'I'd say she's trespassin'.'

'Yeah, but what's she after?'

'Hell if I know.'

'Must be a druggy come lookin' for forgiveness.'

'She better ask in her sweetest voice.'

'Look it, she can't hardly walk.'

'Hey!' they call to her. 'You all right?' But she doesn't turn, doesn't hear them.

'She's headin' straight for it.'

'She must be want'n to touch it.'

'Isn't that against the law?'

In that field of corn, dragging herself the way she is, dressed in her wandering clothes, her hair all astray, she could be some kind of lady scarecrow come to life by strange arts, shocked awake in this tourist trap by the simple emptiness of life, doomed to hunt for love, doomed to scratch an answer in the soil.

'Now what's she doin'?'

'She's turnin' around.'

'She's lookin' right at us.'

'Looks like she's gettin' down to pray.'

'The hell she is.'

'This one needs saving somethin' powerful.'

'I'll be damned. The tramp's pissin'! We gotta get a shot of this.'

'Lucy, cover your eyes!'

'Lester, zoom in!'

'I'm tryin' to, which button is it?'

'Worthless man! Gimmee that goddamn thing!'

And so for all eternity the Van Kleek family of Vermilion County, Illinois, will possess in a cardboard box in their attic physical proof that our haunted rag doll did indeed pass this way. With little more than a feeling to guide her. A folded pamphlet in her backpack. A new name she stole from a dead pop song in a nightmare. Her jeans round her ankles. Her hands on her knees. That cross to the sky. That look on her face. Forever young in that field. Squatting forever in the bright sun.

AT LAST WE MEET

'I'm Mike London with the midday weather summary. Look for the sky to be partly cloudy this afternoon. A chance of scattered showers from Albany south. Rains tapering off by Saturday morning giving way to sunshine and wind most of the weekend. Temperatures in the mid to low sixties. Stay tuned for a solid hour of soft hits and yesterday's favorites on 98.9 FM, The Hawk. Let's start the hour off right. Here's Phil Collins with his 1984 soundtrack smash "Against All Odds".'

'Turn it up,' says Debbie, moved by lust and reflex as she bends to dust off a toy fire truck somebody left in a box by the road this morning.

'You turn it up,' says Black Jesus, stoned on pills in his rocker. 'I don't care about this cheesy crap.'

'That's 'cause you've never been in love,' says his mother with a wistful shake of her gigantic ass. 'You just wait and see.'

Above the Dairy Queen the sky is quiet and grey. Thin clouds sail slow and moody. Two crows chase one another from out of nowhere into the road-side trees, their movements deft, hypnotic in the anxious air.

Just then they hear a motor. A wheezy rattling sound coming close. More like a decrepit chainsaw Debbie sold a Chinese guy a month back than any vehicle they could name.

Then Debbie spies the pink helmet. And as the moped struggles up the road and into her parking lot she feels a vague sense of relief to know it's not that crazy fucker Chinaman returned to cut her up and take his twelve bucks back.

'Who's that?' says Black Jesus.

'Beats me,' says Deb. 'Some chick on a scooter. Looks to me like she's got a screw loose. And I don't mean inside that piece-a-shit she's ridin'.'

The girl plants her feet in the gravel and takes her helmet off and holds it to her chest and looks around as if she'd just been shaken from a long sleep, some breed of skinny amnesiac in greasy blue jeans come to take her bearings in a world she'd like to get to know again.

'Can I help you?' yells Deb, thumbing a white

sticker onto the fire truck and fishing for a black marker with which to write '$8.50 Firm'.

The visitor doesn't answer straight away. She weighs the question the loud lady by the blue tarp just asked and weighing it decides that the kind of help she's really come to need at this hour of her life might be too much to ask of anyone. So what she says is, 'I've gotta find the Mystery Spot. Do you know where it is?'

'Jesus Christ,' says Debbie, getting to her feet. 'That was Old Man Gold's racket. He went belly up, musta been 1998, '99. Served him right, what a sham that place was, water running uphill, my ass. He was a nice man though. Drank like a fish but sweet as pie. When he died the paper said he was a Holocaust survivor, chopped the "Stein" off his name when he got here, never said a word all those years. Hid his tattoo. None of us had the faintest idea what he'd been through.'

'Yes. That's where I'm going. The Mystery Spot. How do I find it?'

Debbie turns to Lionel and whispers, 'Jeez-Louise, sounds like a broken record.' Then back to the girl, 'You ain't gonna find much down there but poison ivy and a summons for trespassin'.'

'The Mystery Spot,' says the stranger. 'Where things are not what they seem. Where just about anything can happen.'

'We got a real live one here, Lionel,' whispers Deb.

A wind hits the tarps and they shudder and shake like dry leaves.

'Who the hell are you?'

'I'm a ballerina,' claims the girl from her steed, her black hair blowing in the driveway. 'I'm known all over the world.'

'That's her, Mom,' whispers Lionel from his rocker, his voice cracked and strange.

'Hold on, honey,' Deb says to him and turns back to the girl in the driveway.

'Go straight down this way,' she yells and points down the highway. 'When you get to the four-way stop hang a left toward Cairo, there's a stoplight and a farm, that's Route 32. You'll go about six, seven miles and you'll see it, just past Mike's Diner on the left.'

'Thank you,' says the runaway and fires up her moped. 'I really need to find it,' she says and puts her helmet on and turns to the road.

'If you see American Karate you've gone too far!' adds Debbie and the girl waves and hits the gas and is gone.

'That was her, Mom.'

'Her who?'

'The dancer.'

'You know that weirdo?'

Black Jesus weighs the question. 'Yes,' he says. 'That's her. The dancer.'

Now Debbie knows what he means. And the old hurt is back in her voice like a flu. 'The day they blew you up?'

'Yeah.'

'The one only you could see?'

'Yeah.'

Another wind hits the tarps and the crows shoot free from the pines they'd harbored in. And there they go dancing out over the road and disappear up the creek, on to Kaaterskill Clove, where ten thousand years ago a most violent water cut this mountain in two like God's slow guillotine, before any coke dealer gnashed his teeth, any flag flew, any boom box spoke for the wind and rain.

PART

TWO

GAY PARIS, NY

Bea Two-Feathers smokes dramatically long cigarettes. The ivory-colored box they come in says
'Extra Light'. Above that there's a silver crown,
jewelled, dazzling, almost sexy, as if this budget
brand might offer the lady who carries them in her
purse some advantage over the rest of the plebs in
her midst, some classier take on life. Bea leans an
elbow against her aluminum walker and blows a
thin stream of smoke through an open window in
her room on the second floor at Serenity Grove.

It must have been the movies. All those beau-
ties in fine things on verandas looking out upon
the lights of LA, lights of Chicago, lights of London. Those slight movements of the wrist, the soft
press of filter to painted lips, the slow trail of that

71

tiny fire's glow in the twilight, like a star to follow. That's when nothing was impossible. Thirteen when she had her first Lucky Strike. The boy down the street had given it to her. The one with the freckles and glowing green eyes, who everyone called trouble, whose dad was gone, who talked to her about prehistoric birds and Japanese knights and how his great uncle on his mother's side was none other than Buffalo Bill Cody. The two of them with the windows rolled up in the cab of the junked truck behind the bungalow he shared with his loose mom. And what a strange feeling when the nicotine hit. After the nausea passed. What a feeling.

'Tell me again about those dinosaur birds.'

'They had a wingspan wider than this truck is long. If you could ride one they could fly you to the North Pole.'

'What about that man who lived in a whale's gut?'

'By candlelight he wrote his life story with a jackknife on the dread beast's stomach wall. He was in there forty days and forty nights, but then he died from suffocation. And when finally the army hunted the whale to the Bermuda Triangle and killed it and cut it open they found the hero's skeleton and all the things he'd written.'

'What do I do with the ashes?'

'You rub it on your jeans for good luck.'

'I'm wearing a dress.'

'Guess that'll have to do.'

'But my folks'll see.'

'Do you want me to tell you what he wrote or not?'

'Sorry. What he write?'

'You really wanna know?'

'Pray tell.'

'The dame he pledged his heart to turned out to be a German spy. She was so good at it he couldn't even hear a trace of Kraut when she spoke American. But because he was a patriot he poisoned her even though he still loved her. And carried her to the sea and threw her in.'

'That's when the whale got him?'

'Jeez, hold your horses.'

'Sorry.'

'Like I was saying, after he threw her in he—'

'Whitey?'

'What?'

'Can you let me out? I think I'm gonna be sick.'

Just then a light knock at her nursing home door.

'Who's that?' she says and throws what's left of her cigarette out the window and makes a fanning motion in the air with her thin hand as if that might make it all go away.

'It's me, Ma.'

'Joe Boy?'

'Who else calls you Ma?'

'Hold on a minute, I'm not decent,' she lies and shuffles on her walker after a spray bottle of Georgia peach air freshener she keeps in a drawer by her bed. Halfway there she loses heart and says to herself, *What's the difference now?* Then calls to her son, 'Okay, come in, I'm fit to behold.'

Entering with a smile on his face her tall son says, 'Well thank you, my queen.'

He looks at her here in the middle of this sad little room and when their eyes meet he finds something there he never saw.

'Were you smoking?'

'Yes, Officer,' she tries to joke. 'You caught me red-handed.'

'What's wrong, Mom?'

Bea doesn't answer right off. She turns her face away and shuffles to the open window. From here she can see the dogwood tree in the yard. Its white flowers, its branches in the easy wind.

'It's caught up with me, Joe Boy.'

The Deputy knows exactly what she means, but all he can bring himself to say is, 'What are you talking about?'

'I didn't wanna tell you till the tests came in and I was sure.'

'You're gonna die?'

'Not this minute.'

'When?'

'That's for the Great Spirit to know, not us.'

'Please, Ma, none of that mumbo jumbo. How long did they say?'

'He said if I do the chemo I have a shot at remission. Or at least kicking around another five, six years.'

'So when do you start?'

'I don't.'

'You gotta be kiddin' me.'

'No, Sir. Honest Injun.'

'How can you joke?'

Now her sideways smirk turns to something else. Now she looks her boy in the face, the afternoon light behind her, the breeze at her long silver ponytail. 'I don't know how else to make you feel better.'

And with that he starts to cry.

'Oh, Joe. Please. I don't wanna make you sad.'

Her tall son couldn't reply if he tried. That ache in his cheeks and throat, that dryness of the tongue and strange play of oxygen we've all come to know.

'The miracles of chemo. I seen enough. Hair of the dog. One kind of death for another. I guess I just figure your time's your time. In here you make friends, guys and gals down the hall. You sit together in the cafeteria, play bridge, crochet, maybe watch a picture in the TV room.' Here Bea takes a pause, and her eyes trail down, moist globes of memory, a war movie there, a chariot race, a starlet dancing barefoot on a windy beach, and says, 'Then one day you look and they're gone.'

Joe moves and sits on his mom's thin bed. Squeak of springs. Soft blanket. Faint smell of fake peach and dying. Now his cell phone rings: *We will, we will rock you.*

'Answer it, Joe Boy.'

He shakes his head, tears down the high bones of his Indian face. *We will, we will rock you.*

'Could be important.'

'It's my girlfriend.'

'The one that bought the Dairy Queen?'

He nods.

'Well, answer it then,' says Bea.

Joe does his best to compose himself. Then he flips the Motorola.

'Hello?'

'Joe?'

'It's me.'

'Don't sound like you.'

'Sorry. I'm visitin' my mom. Must be bad reception.'

'Well we got an emergency down here.'

Like cold water on a town drunk's face the 'E' word snaps the public servant to attention.

'What happened?'

'I apprehended a shoplifter.'

'Are you for real?'

'No time to explain. Just get here ASAP, baby.'

'But I'm here with my mom and she's—'

No need for Joe to finish because Debbie hung up.

'I gotta go, Ma. There's some kind of trouble at the Dairy Queen.'

'Yes. You go. It'll help get your mind off all this.'

'I doubt that very much,' he says and gets to his feet, the springs in the little bed complaining as he rises.

Bending low, he kisses her goodbye and tells her he'll be back in the morning.

When he's halfway out the door Bea warns, 'Be careful, Joe, tonight's a full moon.'

When you gonna stop with that crap? is what he wants to say, but he says, 'Sure thing, Ma. I promise.'

After he's gone the old woman waits a long time at her window. There's birds in the dogwood.

On his way through town Joe spies two drunks fighting tooth and nail in the gravel lot outside Shakespeare's Bar & Grill. He knows them both by heart. Now they're on the ground, rolling and kicking up dust. Work boots and t-shirts and ragged hair. One's got a broken bottle.

Debbie needs me, thinks Joe. *Besides, they'll be kissin' and makin' up before the jukebox can change songs. And if not, let them claw each other to shreds if they want, waste of fresh air the both of 'em.*

Pulling into the Dairy Queen, he notices a strange moped parked by Deb's station wagon, looks like it's been through the war. Sheer habit makes him check his hair in the rear-view before he shuts the cruiser off and gets out. Approaching the scene of the crime he sees a girl squatting in the gravel next to Lionel's rocking chair, a helmet on her head, her face lowered between her knees, both her arms wrapped around them as if to shield herself from a falling sky.

'That you, Joe?' says Lionel from his still rocker.

'It's me, Black Jesus,' says Joe and sees now why the girl hasn't moved. She's handcuffed by her wrist to the back of the chair.

'Where the hell's your mother?' he says.

'Think she went inside,' says Lionel with a stoned smile. 'Didn't know you were bedding down with a crazy lady huh, man?'

'There's gotta be a reason for this.'

'Sure. Just keep your seatbelt on, Geronimo, this is only the tip of the iceberg.'

'Debbie!' yells Joe in the basic direction of the DQ and even before the sound of her name dies under the blue tarps she comes waltzing through the screen door like the lead in a play.

'Well, if it isn't the big bad Deputy. Thought you'd never come. Look what I caught,' she says and points to the girl still frozen there in her desperate pose.

'What's going on here, babe?' says Joe, doing his best to hide the sadness and worry in his voice, the creeping annoyance.

'This freak was trying to steal from us.'

'That's not why I gave you those handcuffs,' says Joe.

'Oh, come on!' barks Lionel. 'I really don't need to hear that, do I? I get enough nightmares as it is.'

'She was stealing a pair of gloves, Joe!'

'A pair of gloves?' says Joe, more annoyed by the moment.

'Those sparkly Michael Jackson ones. Authentic Thriller era. I had 'em marked at eighty bucks!'

'I told her to let her go,' says Lionel. 'This is the dancer. The one I saw when they blew me up.'

'Let's not talk about that now, okay honey,' snaps his mother.

'She came askin' how to get to the Mystery Spot,' says Lionel. 'So Mom told her. Then she came back a little while later and said to me that her hands were cold. She told me to feel them and put one on my face and it was like ice. Mom was in the shower so I told her just to take a pair of gloves. Any ones she wanted.'

'Debbie?'

'What, Joe?'

'Give me the keys for the cuffs.'

'Christ, if you don't believe me see for yourself what they go for on eBay!'

'I don't give a flying fuck about the gloves, Debbie! You should be ashamed. Don't think I don't remember you spending the night in Catskill jail for shoplifting a blender from Jamesway in the nineties. What's that they say? Takes a thief to catch a thief?'

'Joe Two-Feathers! What on earth's gotten into you?'

'You really wanna know?'

'Of course I do, sweet potato.'

'My mom's gonna die. She's got cancer in her lungs. I left her to come down here 'cause I thought you and BJ were in danger. Now just give me the goddamn keys.'

Speechless, Debbie hands him what he asks for. Turning from her, Joe goes to the rocking chair where Lionel sits quietly and gets down on one knee and uncuffs the dancer. She does not move. Hopelessness petrifies, her helmet to her thighs, her arms wrapped tight as a drum, like some odd tortoise they've found.

'Isn't she beautiful, Joe?' says Black Jesus, but nobody answers, all stunned to hear him say such a thing. And then just like a morning glory, the girl lifts her head slowly to stare at the blind Marine, her green eyes like a question, her face framed behind the helmet's shield, her features turned fiercely exotic after a journey of wind and hurt and God only knows what else.

'Are you okay?' says Joe.

'No,' says the dancer turning to him, the sound of this one word alone a three-act tragedy.

'You poor thing,' says Joe. 'What's your name?'

'Gloria,' says Black Jesus. 'Her name's Gloria.'

'Well then, Gloria, let's get you inside. You'll need supper. And a shower. You'll be spending the night here at the Dairy Queen. Among friends. Isn't that right, Debbie White?'

VENICE BEACH, CA

Rough sea. Kids on the boardwalk. Schizophrenic on a bicycle. Tattooed lovers entwined on a picnic table under one of the pagodas, seagull at their feet. Warren Zevon blasting from a yellow convertible turning east on Rose, gone just as quick as he came. And all the vendors are packing up, guy with the sunglasses, guy with the cotton candy, lady with the crystal ball, pretty slow for a Sunday.

Dusk on this weird beachscape. Blanket of rosy haze in the far western sky beyond the blue sea. Here is a place where vanity and beauty and desperation and love and sleaze and new beginnings are all smiling and nailed to one word like a mannequin to a plastic cross in a dream: California.

Ross Klein pays a pretty penny for his place. 13 Brooks Avenue, 2nd floor. A wide-open loft space one of Frank Gehry's rogue protégés allegedly designed. Everything is brushed metal and blacks, occasionally the dangerous color. There, in a corner, lies a girl asleep on his big brass bed. Her strawberry hair all wild on the pillow, her heartbeat soft, her mouth very dry, one of her naked legs like a pale branch growing out from under his sheet, toenails red as new blood. Last night they met at an industry party. He told her his name and she blushed and took a sip of her drink. Then she swallowed and said she was a singer-songwriter from Florida, the Panhandle. He didn't know who she was. And still doesn't. And neither does anyone else.

When Ross Klein woke, his BlackBerry said 6:09 p.m. He tried but he couldn't go back to sleep. The trucks outside, the girl's breathing, the way she ground her teeth.

He threw on a robe and walked across the flat and sat with his naked ass on his favorite couch, its black leather cool to the touch. On a coffee table lay his big headphones and he reached and put them on and switched on a new album he's been putting off listening to. Some indie rockers from Montreal. His editor expects the review by morning. So he started taking notes: sophomoric, overproduced, flippant, somebody's been listening to too much Roxy Music. By track five he was sick to his stomach.

Now he's in the bathroom, his pale feet on the tiles, his robe open in front like a door to his secrets. Here in the big mirror the critic Ross Klein looks the critic Ross Klein up and down. And the two share a strange little laugh.

By the side of the sink is a simple leather shaving kit: gleaming razor and lather brush, worn leather case. Last year they put a handful of Jim Morrison's belongings up for auction online, things from the day they found him dead in that bathroom in Paris. So, being bored one day and high on coke, Ross bid on this haunted tchotchke and won, paying more for it than his cleaning lady makes in a year.

The thin steel handle of the razor has a nice curve, provocative, slight as a dancer. As the man in the mirror lifts it to his face he hears the girl he's never heard of call to him from the bed, her voice like a child faraway.

'Ross,' she coos, but he doesn't answer. Instead he talks to the mirror. '*I'm your private dancer*,' he sings and his eyes are terribly wrong. '*A dancer for money, I'll do what you want me to do. I'm your private dancer, a dancer for money, any old music will do.*'

'Ross?' calls the girl again. 'Come back to bed.'

What this Floridian does not know is that under the bed she finds herself in is a pair of ivory ballet slippers in a box, the pale chalk still on them.

'*I'm your private dancer*,' sings Ross to the mirror. '*A dancer for money*,' he sings and touches the blade to his face. No lather. No matter. He digs in. Cuts in. His face a hated thing. Gouge away. You can gouge away. And down falls his bright blood as from a tap.

GAY PARIS, NY

Waking up on a strange couch is a feeling every lost dreamer knows. Fly on your hand. The uncertain light. Fly on your dry mouth. Seven mild nightmares that run together like wet paints in a new rain, each more mundane than the next. Fly in your wild hair.

What is this place? Smells weird. All this clutter, these boxes, that clothes hanger, that mannequin, her chiffon dress and purple wig, maybe she knows something I don't. It's quiet here. Oh, but there's the sound of a car, and another out there. Now quiet again. A bird. My head hurts. Is that a soda fountain? Why do I feel like I've been here before? Who put this blanket on me?

'Hello?' she says into the musty room, still supine

on the couch, her head turned slightly, her eyes fixed on a darkened window, aluminum mini-blinds.

Nobody answers. But soon she hears footfalls and motion above her. Must be somebody up there. She thinks of the movie Flowers in the Attic and shivers. Now she sits up, trailing her hurt leg slowly, and wraps the knitted blanket around her, its aged purples and pinks and whites giving easily to the contours of her dancer's body.

'Hello?' she says again and cranes her neck in a way that might help her find the source of the racket overhead. Doesn't take her long to spy the hole in the ceiling and the ladder reaching down. And now the big work boots testing the air, learning the way down rung by rung. Those grey sweatpants descending. Like some kind of low-rent astronaut. Oh, but then she knows him. The guy in the rocking chair. Those same silly black sunglasses. Only now not so silly. Because when he says, 'Hi, I didn't know if you'd ever wake up,' he doesn't face her, he faces straight ahead in that pitiful way she's seen acted out a hundred times on TV, the telltale hesitancy, the vague shame and disorientation of the newly blind.

'Do you need help?' she says when he reaches the bottom of the ladder.

To that Lionel White gives a smug little laugh. 'Well, that's ironical,' he says. 'Ain't you the one sleepin' on our couch?'

The girl looks at him there in the poor light, his pale hair awry, his sadness, and pulls her blanket tighter and says, 'I'm sorry. I just thought—'

'You just thought 'cause I'm blind I must be some kinda helpless retard.'

'No. No, not at all. It just seemed like the right thing to say. Sorry, I didn't mean it like that. I guess my right-and-wrong detector's probably been out of batteries awhile. Just ask my leg.'

By reflex she runs her hand down her swollen shin and feels the heat of it, the slow rhythm of its throb, her own little drummer boy, own little war.

'What happened to you?' he asks.

'A lot of things.'

'What's wrong with your leg?'

'I broke it.'

'How?'

'Dancing in the ballet. A horse doctor told me my tibia was fractured. That was a few weeks ago, I guess. Maybe more. God, I must be losing my mind.'

'I think I know what you mean,' says the Marine, still holding onto the ladder for balance.

'Yeah?'

'Yeah.'

'Scary, right?'

He thinks about this a moment, the muscles in his jaw grinding like a motor. Both these broken kids waiting for an answer in this ice-cream-parlor-turned-warped-homestead/junkshop, outnumbered by all the cast-off things that surround them, clothes nobody wants to wear anymore, paintings nobody wants to hang up, memories better kept in a box.

'Yeah,' he says. 'I guess it is kinda scary.' *Sometimes my dreams are so real and bad I shit my tighty whities*, is what he'd like to say. *I don't know why I'm still alive, everything's dark and I'm all doped up and I miss what I can't see. It sounds gay, but I miss the sky. And watching the cars go by on the road. I miss my mom's face*, is what he'd love to say, but he can't.

'I've thought about him a bunch since,' says Gloria.

'Who?'

'The vet who helped me out.'

'Veteran?'

'Veterinarian. Guess we're all animals when it comes down to it.'

'What kind are you?'

'Animal?'

'Yeah.'

'Not sure. I guess I'm a bird. Maybe a swan,' she laughs. 'What about you?'

'A wolf,' says the soldier.

'Really?'

'I don't know. I used to wish I was one. But that's when I was kid,' he says. 'So, what did the doctor do?'

'He put this brace on and told me to stay with him awhile but I didn't really listen.'

'Was he a perv?'

'No. He was a nice man. I just had to go.'

'How come?'

She doesn't answer right away. In her pounding head runs a dim and random montage of things seen and felt on the ragged pilgrimage she made across this land of ours. Land on the brink. Gas pump. All-you-can-eat Chinese food. Truck full of migrants. Abandoned paint factory. Train crossing. Dying bear so beautiful. Jackknife trailer. Sunset to make you cry. Ten thousand small dark birds changing shape in the air as they go like an Etch A Sketch worked by the same playful force that ends the world, same force that shaped it. Cell phone tower disguised as a giant tree. Truck stop. Rodeo. Corn forever. Cows forever. Sunburnt hitchhiker with a dog. Sunrise to challenge all you believe in. Rain. Headlights. RV center. Dirty picture cut into a bathroom wall. Cross to the sky. Big prison on a hill. Carwash. Baseball field. A million pale windmills all turning in the dark.

'I felt like someone was after me.'

'Who?'

'My boyfriend.'

'Do you think he'll find you?'

'I don't know. I'm fucked-up in the head. Somehow I thought I'd be safe if I could just get back to the Mystery Spot.'

'It's not there anymore.'

'I know. I came a long way to find out.'

Here they both breathe and listen. Traffic's picked up out on the road, it's Saturday, cars headed up the mountain, down the mountain. Faintly they hear Debbie outside at her noisy old cash register haggling with some shopper over God knows what amazing triviality.

'Can I come sit by you?' says Lionel out of the blue, as a child might.

'If you want to.'

'Okay.'

And like a little row boat with a hole in it, he pushes off from the ladder and gropes his way through the Dairy Queen towards her voice. With a hurting dizzy head and sleep still in her eyes she watches him come. Almost to the couch, he stumbles on a Ken doll and starts to fall. Gloria gasps out loud and reaches and grabs him just under his armpit as he crashes into the dusty arm of the couch.

'Are you okay?'

'I'm fine,' he says, not as embarrassed as she feared he'd be. And she helps him onto the beat-up cushion beside her.

'Mom's got so much crap lyin' around,' he says with a small awkward smile on his mouth.

'She sure does. Some of it's kinda cool though.'

'You might not think it's cool if you grew up with it.'

'You grew up here?'

'Yeah. No. Well, in a trailer up the road. But she's always had the yard sale. It's our bread and butter. That's what she calls it. Says she'd rather starve than work for The Man. I never really knew what man she was talkin' bout till I went to boot camp. Then I learnt quick.'

'Is that where you got your name?'

'Black Jesus?'

'Yeah.'

He nods and says, 'The Jar Heads named me that. Growin' up I never fit in, so it felt kinda good to have a nickname.'

'Did you fight in Iraq?'

'Sure did.'

'Is that how this happened to you?'

The boy nods his head.

'I'm sorry.'

After a pause he says, 'Don't be sorry. I don't want anybody feelin' sorry for me. A lot worse happened to other guys. If we didn't fight 'em over there we'd end up fightin' 'em at home, in our own backyard.'

The dancer hears this last slogan fall from his mouth as empty and automatic as a parrot, a priest.

'Well, I think you're brave,' she says. 'And who knows, maybe you made it home alive for a reason. Maybe there's something in store for you.'

'Like what?'

'That's the million-dollar question,' she says. 'The big mystery. What happens? Sometimes I think it's the only thing that keeps us going. If we knew every twist of the movie why would we stick around to watch?'

VENICE BEACH, CA

Maybe you've strolled down Rose Avenue on a summer's night, when they flock to this place hoping to fix a love, find a love, end a love. When it's hard to get a table anywhere. When shouts are heard. Or whistles to girls. Or ragged singing on the street corner. When gulls cry. When promises are lost in the mild riot of it all. When the light is dying. Maybe the sea was calm, or maybe it was choppy, or maybe you were too frazzled to measure the wind. No matter. Whatever the details, we can be certain of one thing, you were in earshot of Bebop Billy, the thin junky flutist of Venice.

Having hocked his good flute for dope long ago it would have been his blue recorder you'd of heard, as soft and thin as the man himself, the long notes, the trilled notes all but gone in the roar of waves and cars and cheap revelry. But it was there just the same. And so was he. With an unusual smile on his mouth, and kind, faded eyes, and the dope balloon wrapped up in his pocket, and the tie-dyed turban on his head, and the sick magic in his veins, same thing tonight as he zigzags through the alleys his kind call the speedway, down Rose Court, up Dudley, down Paloma and over to Brooks Avenue blowing tunes to rock to, tunes to heal you, to bless you, to curse your life and blow your mind. It's four in the morning or thereabouts and Bebop sways and his music is pure and he's drawn by a light in the window above. A girl there. Her face in the glass. *She's lost,* thinks Bebop and the notes that escape his recorder now reflect this idea. *Who's she talking to?* he wonders and stops and cranes his neck to watch. It's not long before he knows she's not talking at all. The girl is singing. Silent and lost on the second floor. Not a word makes it out of the locked window, but something about her face and the way she delivers the song breaks Bebop's heart. It's like she knows nobody'll ever hear it. Like her song's stuck there in the window for keeps, or till all these buildings are claimed by the sea. Not long now. So he blows her a junky's prayer and scratches his belly and moves on into the night, where a fix awaits, or something holy, or just another sunrise sleep in the sand.

*

Even though she walked in and found him carving up his face in the mirror. Even though he spat blood onto the tiles and called her a brainless whore and smiled and danced like a rabid gypsy into the next room with the razor aloft. Even though he hasn't showered now for a week and stinks. Even if he's locked the door. And taken the phone off the hook. And doesn't really talk to her much. But talks strange. And into thin air. And mostly it's just other people's songs he parrots, some she's heard and some she hasn't. Even though something inside tells her this might not be the safest scene in the world, Tracy, the would-be next Jewel from Florida (the Panhandle), has remained in this loft with the tastemaker Ross Klein like some breed of attending angel if angels took off their pants and did anything on earth for a shot at the big time.

Maybe this is just his process, she thinks as she hunts through the cupboard for the last box of pasta, last tin of paté. *He's inspired. How else could he write those mind-blowing pieces he's so famous for? This is how real artists get their feelings out. A bit of madness to spice up the broth. Wow, I like the sound of that, did I come up with that myself? Must be rubbing off. Here I am right on the front line. I wouldn't be surprised if he writes me into his next blog. If Daddy could see me now. 'Don't you know that you are a shootin' star?' we'd sing in his*

*truck when I was a tadpole. 'All the world will love
you just as long as you are a shooting star.'*

And the vintage Motown ceiling fans he bought
from Berry Gordy's accountant spin round and
round. And the false breezes they conjure play at
the hair and face and torso of the man lying there
on the floor, his spine against the oval rug, his robe
wide open. Eyes wide open.

Having laid his spooky razor aside in favor of
other charms, Ross has cultivated a fairly impres-
sive beard, high to the cheekbones, all down his
throat, and tawny in color. Yesterday in his pacing
he passed a framed photograph of John Lennon and
Phil Spector in some black-and-white control room
somewhere in time, and passing them he saw his
own face in the reflection of the glass and was start-
led. Because at that angle, obscured in the light that
way, it was also his father's face. The mean eyes. The
beard. The same way he knew him when they spent
that long month on his yacht. November 1984. The
date seared in the boy's mind on account of how
his dad kept him up late election night by the loud
crackly radio in the cabin waiting at the edge of
their seats for each state to weigh in on the triumph
that was to be the dawn of Ronald Reagan's second
term in office.

*'An actor,' said his father in the harsh light below
deck after all the votes were in. 'A Californian. One*

of our own. A hero straight outta storyland. That's just what it's gonna take to win this country back its balls. You know what I mean when I say balls don't you, son?'

Here the boy looked the man in the face and it seemed to him that the dark blond beard he wore was a disguise, something from a picture book, something to hide behind, beyond which might lie a fantastic world, maybe where the wild things are, maybe a place where all fathers are good fathers and wise. Then the boy looked down at his little penny loafers and started to cry.

'Jesus Christ. Your mother's molded you into quite the pussy, hasn't she?'

'You still didn't tell me where she is,' wept the child.

'She left us.'

'When's she coming back?'

'Coming back? She's not coming back. Not till hell freezes over. Not till a field of roses grows all the way down Sunset Strip. There's Jew lawyers making sure of it.'

'Where'd she go?'

'You really wanna know?'

'Yes,' sobbed the child into his hands. This child eight years old. This thirty-foot Hatteras rocking in the cold night waters.

'She started fucking some gypsy faggot of a singer. Bobby something. Some B-rate Donovan she met at *a party in Laurel Canyon last year when I was away on business in New York. Shame on me for trying to make an honest woman out of her. I guess this is my penance for making a kid with a go-go dancer. Sheila. Stock name for any low-life rag doll from any old shithole in the Midwest. My mother, your grandmother—rest her soul—said it best: Love is a fairy tale, let's leave love to Hollywood, when it comes to marriage the trick is in the breeding, and that girl isn't fit to scrub our floors.'*

What hidden savagery can live in the hearts of the painfully rich. A secret saved for the country club toilet. And Ross Klein, lying pale in his open robe on a sweaty rug, growing the beard his father handed down to him, is heir to such things. Should he wish to be.

But how could he forget the quiet beauty with the black braid? The scared and haunted mom he'd not see again. Sheila chasing songs. The faint patchouli she wore. The lisp when she talked, first voice he knew, and for the first few years of his life he would have sworn the billion other tongues on earth were flawed, not hers. She played him her best tapes on the 8-track player in the porch window of their place in the Hills. Van the Man and Jackson Browne and Tim Buckley and Joni and The Byrds. Carole King and Sweet Baby James and Judy Collins and Earth, Wind & Fire till the tapes broke. Songs that told of the life she gave up to live in this gigantic house. The boy in her lap rocking softly in the piney air when she'd sing along and they'd watch the city traffic struggle in the twilight down there, all the lights of Los Angeles blinking on through the haze like phosphorous life in a nameless sea of want and pending disaster.

But boys turn to men. And men litter their worlds with pain. Ross on the floor. His world a falling world. His glassy eyes on the ceiling. His ticking heart, blue-black and hidden like a mine.

GAY PARIS, NY

Joe's pants are on the floor of Debbie's bedroom in the back of the Dairy Queen. A dusty broken walk-in cooler six months ago, this ten-by-twelve space, got to through a heavy metal door behind the old kitchen in back, has since been reinvented as a veritable love den complete with candles, vaguely Eastern tapestries above a twin futon, baby oil on the nightstand, Rite Aid brand. It's just barely dawn, a Greyhound bus passes out on the main road in the half-dark, Deb snores lightly by his side and the cell phone in the pocket of his Dickies on the carpet sings a muted *We will, we will rock you.*

'Joe here.'

'Joe boy?'

'Who is this?'

'Who else calls you Joe Boy?'

'Why you callin' so early, Mom?'

'I want to go to the drive-in one more time before I die.'

'You're not gonna die, Ma.'

'Oh yes I am. I hate to be a party pooper but so are you. And that strange big bird you've shacked up with. And every other blessed creature in the universe one day or another. And my day's just around the bend, whether you like it or not. No sense moping about it. That's why *I'm singin' in the rain,*' sings Bea Two-Feathers.

'But isn't there something we can do to—'

'Singin' in the rain. I'm not gonna be one of those sad sacks who fights tooth and nail for nothing. I sincerely hope I just clap off like the clapper the day he comes knocking.'

'Who?'

'The guy with the cycle. Death. The Boatman. Ferryman. Whatever you wanna call him. All I want is to go to the friggin' drive-in movies one last time and that goddamn Director Steve won't grant me a day pass.'

'Why the hell not?'

Debbie stirs beneath the sheet. 'Who you talkin' to, baby?'

Joe covers the phone with his long hand and whispers, 'My mom. I think she's losing her marbles.'

'I heard that.'

'Shit. Sorry, Mom. I'm just worried about you.'

'So then get your ass down here and have a talk with this Nazi director.'

'Okay, I'll be down, just let me get my pants on,' says Joe and hangs up.

'Don't you dare put those pants on yet,' says fat Deb. 'You hear me, Tonto?'

Just upstairs in the crow's nest, the young Marine sweats in his blanket with his knees drawn up to his chest, his maimed eyelids twitching, his pale stoned head host to a shifting slideshow of horrors not seen on CNN. Not seen on FOX. Babar crushed against his armpit where elephants can't forget.

He can hear shells falling three miles to the west, a dull simple rhythmic barrage he's come to regard as an unlikely comfort in this alien land. He's not supposed to be here. Not in this country and not in this empty lot. He's slunk off to hide awhile, to sit with his back against a wall, his gun on his lap and his head tilted back in an uneventful corner of this ruined capital where he might find a little rest from the fight, the shrill finite stabbing in his temples, the grinding of his jaw, a built-in standard of confusion, the whole of his half-hearted liberating force getting nowhere quick.

They're building a Burger King here. See the signposts they drove into the ground. It boasts the name of the contractor awarded the job, 'Liberty Corp.: Working hand in hand with your community to build a brighter tomorrow'. A lean yellow dog runs from the shadows and rattles a paint can and it scares Black Jesus half to death. The slightest unexpected thing. The smallest crash nearby. A bottle breaking. Kids throwing stones. Maybe a Datsun backfires. All these things will make him gasp, make him shake, send the coldness up his back.

He's not supposed to be here. Not supposed to see what he saw.

'Mike London here with your 98.9 FM, The Hawk morning weather. Unseasonably cool today but sunny and clear in the higher elevations. Highs in the upper sixties. Not a cloud in the sky. I see a warm front moving up the coast from the Carolinas but we won't feel the effects of that till the weekend. More updates every hour, on the hour. Now it's time for On This Day as we take a quick ride down memory lane with some fun facts from the internet. It's the 11th day of August. So let's start this one off right. On this day in 1956, Elvis Presley releases 'Don't Be Cruel', hell yeah. On this day in 1971, construction begins on the Louisiana

Superdome. On this day in 1978, the world mourns the death of Pope Paul VI and legionnaires' disease bacteria was isolated in Atlanta, Georgia. On this day in 1866, the world's first roller rink opens in Newport, Rhode Island. On this day in 1991, space shuttle Atlantis 9 lands back to earth. On this day in 1982, the US performs a nuclear test in the Nevada desert. On this day in 1976, Keith Moon, drummer for The Who, collapses and is hospitalized in Miami. On this day in 1980, the Yanks' Reggie Jackson hits his 400th home run. On this day in 1999, the Salt Lake City tornado tears through the downtown district killing one. And on this day in 1965, The Beatles movie Help opens in New York City. So I hasten to add that this day is as good as any to say something from the heart, in these tough times we could all use a little Help, so here you go Catskill region, and remember: I really appreciate you sticking round.'

'I lost my virginity to this song,' says Debbie White to a bewildered customer, an old lady in a platinum blonde wig who's come to declare that one of the antique rings for sale in Deb's jewelry case is indeed her wedding band and she wants it back.

'You gotta be kiddin' me,' Debbie tells her. 'I traded a pair of 180 Dolomite skis for that ring with a kid from up the mountain, musta been last November.'

'When Harold left me I didn't know what else to do,' says the woman. 'I was all alone with the kids and the bills piled up so I took it to a pawnbroker in Albany.'

'Ain't that a shame.'

'So *quick bright things come to confusion,*' says the woman, looking off in the distance.

'What the hell's that supposed to mean?'

'It's Shakespeare, you dimwit. Harold was so fond of poetry. It's how he weaseled his way into my pantyhose.'

'That's funny, we got a Shakespeare's right down the street, and there you'll find comedy,' Deb takes a pause for dramatic effect, '. . . and tragedy.'

'And maybe a busted lip if you mouth off,' chimes in Lionel.

The octogenarian looks at the kid in the rocking chair, smiles a wry smile and says, '*Cupid is a knavish lad, thus to make poor females mad.*'

'Okay lady, listen,' says Deb, 'I'll give you a ten per cent senior citizens discount. That's the best I can do.'

'What if I could prove it was mine?'

'Finders keepers.'

'Have a heart,' pleads the woman.

'Thirty-one fifty-five. Take it or leave it.'

'What if I call the cops?'

'Go right ahead. Oh, wait. On second thought,

you don't have to waste the quarter. Here he comes now.'

Joe slams the sheriff's cruiser in park and jumps out, it doesn't take a mind reader to see he's upset.

'If we're done here I've got to tend to my man,' says Deb and the lady spews out a string of out-dated cuss words and looks at the gold ring in the glass case there as lost and tarnished as the way she feels about the plot of her own life, the present state of the USA. Then she skirts round the approaching Joe Two-Feathers and gets in her Mercury Sable and drives away.

'What was that about?' says Joe.

'Nothing,' says Deb. 'What happened at the old folks home? Are they gonna let your mom out?'

'That Director Steve is a real son of a bitch.'

'I guess that means no.'

'Did you know he's a sexual weirdo? Yeah. He talked about it like he was telling me the scores to a Mets game. Orgasmic liberation. Anal. Bisexuality. Butt beads. Orgies. Sat yapping at me in his office for half an hour. I shit you not. Told me he's tired of his wife. Go figure. Told me how he's filed for divorce on the grounds that she tried to poison him with an ambrosia salad.'

'Is that the one with fruit and marshmallows?'

'I thought it was whip cream!' shouts Black Jesus, oddly passionate about this single ingredient.

'Beats the hell out of me,' continues Joe. 'It's not important. The important piece of info is that this guy is fucked-up. Mental. And this is who we got taking care of our parents in their twilight years? He bit and sucked on his pencil and told me now he's got the hots for the divorce attorney he hired. Terry Lipbaum.'

'A man?'

'Yes, Black Jesus. A man. Can you believe that freaky shit?'

'So what's the big deal about letting your mom go watch a drive-in movie?'

'He says her day trip privileges have been suspended till the staff review her case.'

'What the hell for this time?'

'Gambling.'

'Shit, bingo again?'

'Horses.'

Debbie can't help but laugh. And by now Gloria has abandoned the chest of drawers and crept closer with her National Geographic and taken a seat on the ground next to Lionel's rocker so as to be sure not to miss a word.

'She's got a friend at the OTB who's been feeding her the inside dirt on races, doped-up thorough-breds, hot jockeys, etc.,' says Joe. 'Come to find out she's been making a killing on the other residents in the TV room after dessert and coffee.'

Gloria raises her hand like a kid in class and waits to be called upon.

Joe sees her and nods to Debbie and Debbie turns and sees the hand up and says, 'What, Gloria?'

'I want to meet your mom, Joe. She sounds incredible.'

'Visiting hours stop at four,' says the Deputy. 'Just watch out for that pervert. His office is on the ground floor.'

'Can I bring Lionel?'

'Black Jesus,' says the blind boy.

'I don't know,' says Debbie. 'He hasn't gone anywhere on his own since he's been home.'

'He won't be on his own if he's with her,' says Joe.

'You really think it's a good idea, honey?' Deb squints at Joe.

'I think she'd like it if some young people came to see her. She still thinks she's a teenager anyhow by the crazy shit she gets into. And she's gonna need cheering up after I drop this no-drive-in-movie bomb on her.'

'How'm I gonna get there?' Lionel wants to know.

'First things first is you gotta get up from that chair,' says Gloria rising to her feet.

'But I like my chair. It's close to the ground if I fall.'

'You're not gonna fall.'

'You never know. I'm S-T-O-N-E-D,' he says, drawing out each letter slower than the last.

'Stoned?'

'Stone Cold Steve Austin, Ma. I took three pills with a Mountain Dew right when I woke up.'

'You're supposed to just have half a one in the morning and the other half with dinner, pumpkin,' says Deb, a little scared to upset him.

'Yeah, but you didn't see what I dreamed last night.'

Everyone is quiet after that. His declaration hangs in the air like burnt brakes on the mountain road. The radio plays. He makes a mark in the gravel with his work boot. Down at the stoplight someone lays on their horn.

Then Gloria says, 'So I guess that's a yes? Great. It's the big cement building with all the windows, right Joe?'

'Yeah. Just down the road behind all those trees in the back of the field past Shakespeare's. It's an easy walk.'

'I ain't walkin' nowhere,' says Lionel, his big black glasses gleaming.

'That's what I thought you'd say,' smiles Gloria. 'Debbie, is it okay if I use that yarn?' she asks, pointing to a plastic box full of jean patches and thread and balls of wool.

'Not the aqua-blue stuff.'

'How 'bout the gold one?'

'Go ahead,' says Deb, newly enthused by the idea of Gloria and Lionel's visit to Serenity Grove if it helps her prospects of getting some alone-time with her warrior poet. 'Just bring it back,' she says. 'Good yarn don't grow on trees.'

'Thanks,' says the dancer. Then to Lionel, 'It's time you got outta that friggin' chair. There's a big world out there.'

'Yeah, look what good it's done me.'

Without answering she moves and squats and grabs the yarn and walks back to the Marine.

'Hold still,' she says and bends and begins wrapping it around his torso, tight around his sweatshirt.

'What are you doing?'

'Taking your sorry ass for a walk.'

Normally his mom would object to any of this nonsense relating to her son's happiness and general security, but love's got her by the cash register locked with the tall Indian in what looks like a pro-wrestling hold. And they're whispering dirty things, tongues in ears.

Now Gloria trots over to her trusty moped, the ball of gold yarn unraveling behind her, and ties the last of it to the rusted bar above the back tire. Then she deftly straddles the machine and throws her helmet on and turns the key and lurches forward, pulling Black Jesus from his rocker, as obedient as any sleepwalker, arms out and his legs dancing a rusty two-step.

And off they go, out of the parking lot and onto the waiting roadside, two kids, nothing much to lose, tied to each other by more than just yarn somehow.

VENICE BEACH, CA

By this hour of day Bebop Billy is certainly high as a
News 10 helicopter. Out at the far end of the boardwalk he sways to and fro studying the wide blue
living emptiness that rolls out before him. After a
while, he lifts the plastic recorder to his mouth and
blows a slow lament for the world he lives in, the
country he stands at the edge of.

What are we headed toward? he wonders as he
fingers the holes, lifting, landing, lifting again. *How
will it all play out?*

When the tune is through he breathes and closes
his eyes, feels the warm drugs inside him, the warm
ocean air on his face. Turning his head slowly to
one side he sees he's got company. It's the junky

transvestite everybody calls Lady Di. Bebop's seen her plenty of times round the speedway but oddly the two have never shared a word, a needle. No telling how long she's been standing here, watching, listening. Wearing a purple boa about her brown neck and a green see-through sun visor on her head and a t-shirt that says CANCER above a big red smiling cartoon crab, she purses her lips and claps a soft little clap, the kind commonly mustered by aristocracy after they've been mildly entertained, maybe a yawn would follow, maybe a paper fan in this heat.

'You in showbiz?' asks Lady Di.

'No,' says Bebop. 'I'm camera shy.'

'Shit, that makes you one in a million in this tacky ass jungle nine oh two one oh.'

'How 'bout you?'

'Showbiz? Shit, I was almost a big eff-in' star one time. Had a record deal and all that. Opened up for Fester Pussycat.'

'What happened?'

'I don't know. I guess you could say it went down the tubes. That's the easy way to say it. Who can ever really pinpoint the moves that lead us to our own disaster? Shit, that would make a hot chorus. You could use that in one of your songs, man. Just cut me in on the royalties.'

'Do you miss it?'

The tranny takes a moment to reflect. She's tall. The three-day-old make-up on her face makes her look like a rodeo clown who just checked himself into a hospital after a significant bender.

'I miss the show,' says the tranny. 'The roar of the crowd. When they scream for you it's like nothing else on earth. You're God for an hour and a half. You know how you know you're doing a good show?'

'How?'

'It's when the girls start throwing their panties at the stage. You know how you know when you're doing a fabulous show?'

'No.'

'It's when they throw the panties and the panties stick to you like glue. That's how you know you're really on fire. Why'd you choose the recorder, man? Kinda gay, don't you think?'

'Look who's talking.'

'Take that back! This creature you see before you is not gay by any stretch of the imagination. He's just caught between two worlds, baby. But never mind that. All I'm saying is I'd love to see you pick up a Flying V or something. Something with some balls.'

Bebop looks down at the blue recorder in his hands. *What are we headed toward?* Then he looks out to the sea. *How does it all play out?* His high is waning, his stomach a little uneasy.

'I've gotta go,' he tells the tranny. 'So long,' he says and turns away and starts down the boardwalk.

'Hey, I'm sorry, baby,' calls Lady Di.

Billy doesn't hear him because he's blowing on the recorder again. A tune to fix the evening. A tune to bring a scary rain. Just a tune to fill the emptiness that gnaws.

'I didn't mean it, man! That flute's the perfect thing for you. Let's be friends, okay? You're beautiful in every way! Look at you. You're like the Pied Piper with that thing. Fooling all the rats. Leading all the rats out to drown!'

Half an hour later Bebop's lying in the speedway. Spine on the asphalt. Happy eyes on a sick sky. A red balloon in his grimy pocket, his poison, his medicine. Half the contents of that balloon in his bloodstream once again and he strikes the piper's pose and blows a hapless prayer into the warm wind.

'Do you hear that, sweets?' says Tracy on the black sofa. 'I think it's coming from down on the street,' she says and gets up and prances to the window. 'I heard it once or twice before. I think you were sleeping. It's really pretty. But it's just as sad. Isn't that weird?'

'*Oh you pretty things,*' croaks a nude Ross Klein off-key, smoldering on the other side of the apartment. '*Don't you know you're driving your mommas and poppas insane?*'

'Umm, baby? All these lyrics are really brilliant, and enlightening and everything, but sometimes I just wanna talk to you. The real you. I'm sorry. Don't be mad. It's my fault. Maybe I'm missing the point.'

'*Let's give them something to talk about. A little mystery to figure out. How about love?*'

'Really?' says the girl, turning from the window to face him. 'You wanna talk about love?'

'Sure. Why not? But first I need you to do something for me.'

'Anything.'

'Where's your cell phone?'

'I turned it off like you told me to. And threw the battery out the window.'

'You don't have to lie to me. I saw you sending a text yesterday. It's okay. Just go get it. I want you to make a phone call for me.'

The girl lowers her strawberry blonde head like a shamed child and walks back over to the sofa and squats in her sundress and fishes under the leather cushions for her Nokia. There it is.

'Who am I calling?' she says once the flip-top's open to her view.

'Three two three, seven seven nine, four four four six.'

'Is it a takeout place? I really hope so. We haven't really eaten anything for a while.'

'Don't worry. Just call and ask for Desiree.'

The girl looks at him there by the stove. His ragged beard. His wild eyes. *Don't argue with him,* she thinks. *He must have some greater plan in store. Like those TV preachers back home,* she decides.

'Three two three, seven seven nine . . . ?' She dials and waits for the last bit.

'Four four four six,' he says and steps backwards and hoists himself up onto the big iron stovetop like some prehistoric gymnast and watches her dial the rest.

'Cat House, Brown Shugah at your beck and call,' says a woman's voice, loud music in the background.

'Hi, is Desiree there?'

Nothing from the other end, just a guitar solo screaming.

'Hello? I'm looking for someone named Desiree.'

'Yeah, you and everybody else down here,' says Brown Shugah. 'We ain't seen her since just after Easter. She covered my shift so I could take my mom to church. You know where she is? You best to tell me if you do.'

'Umm . . . no. I'm calling on behalf of a friend,' says Tracy, glancing up at Ross to find a wretched smile on his mouth.

'Oh. Now I get it,' says the voice.

'Get what?'

'I know exactly what friend you callin' on behalf of. Put him on the phone.'

'I'm sorry,' says the girl, her free hand pinching her dress material, twisting it tight. 'I must have the wrong number.'

'No, you got the right number, bitch. He knows it by heart. Used to call down here every night askin' for her. You tell that creepy motherfucker I know he did somethin' to my girl. Shit, he probably got her hanging in a meat locker downtown. No, better yet, had her hacked up in a million pieces for shark bait when he takes his friends out on Daddy's yacht.'

Tracy from Florida is speechless. She looks at Ross Klein and lifts her cell phone aloft, a searching ripple in her forehead. But he just smiles that poltergeist smile. And crosses his pale legs in a provocative sweep while Brown Shugah's tirade spews quietly into the stale air.

'Best to pack your bags right now if you know what's good for you, baby. Silver spoon motherfucker. Lyin' ass motherfucker. You tell him Brown Shugah's got his number. Freddy Krueger motherfucker.'

And all Tracy wanted to do today was talk about love.

GAY PARIS, NY

'Are you seein' what I'm seein'?' says the alcoholic.

'Does a bear shit in the woods?' says his buddy.

The two of them squint in the late morning sun on Shakespeare's porch, a can of Coors Lite in each of their hands, a cigarette dangling from the tall one's mouth.

'I'll be damned, that's that war hero kid of fat Debbie White.'

'War hero my ass. Look at that skinny pussy, getting drug along Route 23A by some skank on a Vespa.'

'You be careful what you say, Dennis. I don't have to remind you how I went to Nam and got shot at for six hundred days by a bunch of crazy little rice farmers on speed when you went to Canada to live on some Harry Krishna sex commune. That kid there,' he points to Black Jesus by the roadside, stumbling with his arms out, as if the mounted stranger he's tied to were some witch or healer guiding him down to the river in his dark shades and sorrow, hellbent to get him in the water and wash away the terror so that once again he might see. 'That kid lost his friggin' sight in the godforsaken desert so that you can sit around in this piece-a-shit town and drink yourself shitty and go to Wal-Mart and buy a steak and jerk off to American Idol at night on your couch without fear some towel-headed dune-coon's lookin' in yer window with a RPG. That kid might be a few cards shy of a full house but you can bet yer bottom dollar he's got twice the set of balls you got.'

'How do you know, faggot? You been watchin' me at the urinal?'

Here the tall man patiently bends and squats and sits his beer can on the concrete stoop. On his way back up he pivots and strikes with his fist and catches the draft dodger square in the mouth.

Now blood runs down his eagle t-shirt. Now he retaliates. Now they're rolling and kicking in the sandy lot. One jabs his finger in the other's eye. They curse. They grunt. This is not a new fight. Nothing new about blood and sand.

*

The lady at the front desk looks at them warily and chews her sugarless gum. Then she hands them the clipboard to sign and tells them where they can find Bea Two-Feathers: Room 11, 2nd floor.

Gloria knocks at the door. The knock produces a single muted word in the small room beyond, 'Shit' by the sound of it. The visitors hear movement, light footfalls, the sound of an aerosol can. After a little while Bea turns the knob and stands there in her nightgown, the long white braid falling down her breast, an uncanny look upon her face, as if she might have expected these strays to come calling.

'Bea?'

'You must be the ballerina Joe Boy told me about.'

'Gloria,' says Gloria, the white lie surrounding her life and livelihood sounding stranger to her ears by the day.

'And Black Jesus, I presume?'

'At your service,' says the soldier, high as a kite and oddly invigorated by the forced march he just endured.

'Well, do come in,' says Bea. And as they smile their awkward smiles and slip past her into the room, she lingers to shoot a suspicious glance down the empty hall, now to the left, now to the right, eyeing the vicinity for spies. None there, so slowly she backs into her world and shuts the door.

'Where would you like us to sit, Bea?' asks a polite Gloria, something about the look in the old woman's eyes giving the runaway the sense that maybe she's in the presence of something rare, someone not unfamiliar with the supernatural arts of mischief and unfiltered glee, the magic of far-flung daydreams, the magic of loneliness.

'Sit wherever you like, dears,' says Bea in her soft raspy voice like a fifties movie queen. 'I for one like it by the window, never know what you're gonna see out there.'

Gloria smiles and helps Lionel to the small bed against the wall, hand on his forearm, hand on the small of his back. Slow and easy. And once he's settled, his hands crossed in his lap, Gloria takes a seat beside him and says, 'I'm sorry they won't let you out. I know how it feels to be trapped. Worst feeling in the world.'

'Oh, Joe Boy musta spilt the beans about my very unglamorous house arrest. Please don't feel bad for me, I brought it upon myself I suppose.'

'How?'

'Reach underneath the mattress and I'll show you.'

'Where?'

'Right between your legs.'

Gloria does as she's told.

'Deeper,' says Bea, and soon the girl feels the cool thin metal there and pulls the tarnished cigarette case from its stash spot.

'Smoking? That's what got you in trouble?'

'You can say that again. Big trouble.'

'Joe said it was gambling.'

'Smoking, gambling, drinking, six of this and one half dozen of the other. I do whatever I want. I'm a free agent. In my mind at least. And that Doctor Mengele downstairs can't stomach it, the weird pervert.'

'I thought his name was Director Steve,' says a bewildered Lionel.

'It is,' says Bea. 'Doctor Mengele was an evil Nazi who did gruesome experiments on living people. Sometimes I get them confused. Gloria, would you mind?' she says, a simple toss of her chin carrying with it one pure and unmistakable meaning.

Gloria takes a cigarette from the case and hands it to Bea and Bea bends and reaches down into her white shoe and produces a wooden match and rises and puts her hand out the window and strikes it on the same concrete wall that hems her in, then brings the match in carefully, so as not to kill the flame, aware of its delicacy more now than ever in her life, and fires the long thin smoke between her lips.

After a few good pulls she says, 'It must be fun being a ballerina.'

'Yeah,' says Gloria. 'You know, it has its ups and downs. A lot of practice. A lot of traveling. I'm taking a little break now 'cause I hurt my leg.'

'She's the best,' says Lionel. 'Don't let her fool you. I seen her do it.'

Gloria takes a glance at the Marine but says nothing.

'I used to dance,' says Bea. 'All night to the big band. Then when I met Joe's father he taught me rain dances. He was a full-blooded Mohawk, you see. And I learnt a war dance. And a special fertility dance. Though I'm sure he made that one up to get me out of my knickers. Guess it worked like a charm,' she laughs.

'What was Joe like when he was a kid?' asks the girl.

'Not much different from most kids, I guess. But I know he hated being part Indian. I'd hear the other boys say stuff like mixed-breed and Geronimo and sometimes he'd come home upset and with marks on his clothes, sometimes his face.'

'He gave me his tomahawk,' says Lionel.

'You must be kidding?'

'No. It was a gift.'

'He must really like you. That old thing was his pride and joy. In those days there was no Nintendo.

No web, or whatever they do now. The kids played Good Guys and Bad Guys, all of them running though the woods and across the road without a care, Cops and Robbers, Kill the Commie, Cowboys and Indians. And of course the Cowboys always won. Look at the Marlboro Man.'

'Yeah, but Interstate fucked him right up!' shouts Lionel. 'Killed him fair and square. I was eleven, saw it with my own eyes.'

'Well, then look at the Wild West. You ever been on a reservation? It's enough to break your heart.'

'I rode past one on my way here, but I didn't stop,' says Gloria. 'Somewhere in Oklahoma. Or maybe Michigan. There was a big wooden sign that said the name of the place but I forget it. Something Nation. All I remember is the fence. It seemed to stretch on for hours.'

'A fence for what?' says Black Jesus.

Bea Two-Feathers sucks at her cigarette. Then she says, 'A fence to keep in the sadness.'

And that's all she says, looking out the open window where she stands, waning, defiant, very pretty. Every inhale her delight. Every inhale her creeping death. A warm late summer breeze plays at the branches of the dogwood she loves. Robin in the grass. Dumpster at the edge of the lot. A thin diagonal wisp of hanging carcinogen easy to mistake as a summer cloud lingers far in the sky above, the faint spectre of a jet plane's path, jet plane long gone by.

'Will we leave something behind?' says Bea at last.

'I'm not sure what you mean,' says the girl.

The rain-dancer points to that fading plume in the sky. The stripper gets up from the bed and joins her at the window.

'I don't really know, Bea. I'm sorry. I wish I could say.'

'Maybe there'll be a trail left to show our steps when we're gone. You know, Gloria? Like Hansel and Gretel in the book. Breadcrumbs. The turns we take. A fork in the road. The different ways home.'

'I don't think I really know what home even means.'

'I used to think I did,' says Bea. 'Till I ended up in a HOME. Pretty funny, huh?'

Gloria makes a small obligatory laugh and turns her head from the window to check on Lionel.

He's fast asleep on the woman's bed. Lying on his side with his arms to his heart and his legs drawn up in that pose we all know, and knew, even before the first breath of air came to sting our lungs.

'Is he okay?' asks Bea.

'Not right now. But I think he will be. I want to help him if I can.'

'What's wrong with him?'

'The military's got him on some crazy dope. But I get the feeling it's hurting him more than it's helping.'

'Poor kid. He doesn't look like he'd harm a fly.'

'I know what you mean. I don't think we can even try and imagine what he's been through.'

'Hell on earth,' Bea says and blows a thin mouthful of smoke through the open window. 'Do you mind if I light a candle for him when you leave?'

'What for?'

'To ask the Great Spirit for healing. Some call it the Big Medicine.'

'Sure. That would be nice.'

'And one for your leg?'

'Don't worry about me. I'm okay.'

'No you're not. You're just like me. You'd run yourself into the ground for everybody else before admitting you're in the slightest bit of trouble.'

'Okay, fine. Do one for me too,' says the stripper. 'But light his first.'

Bea smiles and the two of them gaze out the window to the yard, the dogwood, the sky. Whatever ragged line the jet plane left in its wake is nearly gone now. A pale trace here, pale trace there.

'Maybe home is a whole lot different from what we've dreamt it up to be,' says the old woman, finished with her cigarette, her white braid frayed and blowing, a feather pinned to the back of her head.

'It can't just be a name painted on a mailbox. Or a mortgage paper. Or a new bedroom set from Sears. What if all it is is a place where we feel okay? Somewhere we can be whatever we want. And everyone we love is just a tin can telephone call away.'

On their way back to the Dairy Queen, Gloria takes them on a detour. Turning at the white church they make their way down the hill, across the tannery and up Mill Road along the creek. They go at a snail's pace. No yarn to drag the soldier this time. In fact, he walks at her side, where she barely works the throttle. Cars pass them by and necks crane, some folks wave and some don't.

'Where are we going, Gloria?'

'I want to take you down by the water.'

'What for?'

'I'm not really sure yet.'

Half a mile later, she parks the moped in the roadside dirt and takes his hand and leads him down a littered path to an unmistakable Gay Paris landmark. The Swinging Bridge. An old-style narrow cable affair with a rotting wooden deck hanging thirty feet over the rushing creek below. It got its name because it swings in a good wind, and moans, and creaks as you step lightly across. Tales of young sex and death abound. Just before they get to it

Lionel steps on a beer can and the sudden metal noise underfoot freaks him out.

'It's okay,' says the girl, his hand in hers. 'It's just a piece of trash some moron left.'

Halfway across the fabled span she halts their advance saying, 'Wait.'

'Wait for what? We better get across this crazy fucker thing before something happens.'

'Just listen.'

'I knew a kid who got caught between the boards one time and—'

'Shhhh. Please. Just listen.'

'Listen for what?'

'Nothing in particular. Just sounds. Just life.'

Thirty seconds later he says, 'I hear you breathing.'

'Lucky for me. What else?'

The boy lifts his face, black shades gleaming off the water in the noonday sun.

'The creek,' he says. 'It's really moving.'

'Can you see it in your head?'

'Yes.'

'Good,' smiles Gloria. 'That makes me happy.'

They stand here awhile. The bridge rocks gently, called to life by their movements, the slightest change in posture. This creekwater runs to the Hudson. The Hudson runs to the sea.

'Gloria?'

'What?'

'I think I hear my heart.'

Ten minutes later they're sitting side by side at the water's edge, their socks and boots on the stones, their pale feet in the cold stream. The sycamore seeds we call helicopters falling and spinning down into the current to dance away. They sit in silence. Then the fire whistle blows noon, its reliable and distant wail a built-in comfort to the boy. Twelve times it cries, the last one trailing off.

'We gotta get her out of there,' says Gloria.

'Who?'

'Bea Two-Feathers.'

'Jailbreak?'

'I'm not sure yet.'

'Gloria?'

'Yeah?'

'I got your back.'

'Ditto kiddo.'

VENICE BEACH, CA

Tracy makes a noise like a hurt dolphin and her drum-tight eyelids quiver, her hair flung wild on the pillow. She's dreaming of home. *The plastic music box in her tiny bedroom at Dad's trailer with the perverted elf on top that twirls to the narcotic tempo of 'O Night Divine' when she winds it up. Maybe songs aren't meant to be kept in boxes. And maybe girls aren't either. A balmy wind comes into the room through a crack in the window, silent from the Gulf of Mexico, and through the wall she hears the TV say, 'Seven out of ten Americans believe in some form of extra-terrestrial life.' Then the TV says, 'An Orlando mother drowns her four-year-old in a bathtub to protect a secret.' Then later it says, 'New study finds excess body fat linked to growing*

135

number of new cancer cases in this country. Obesity: trend or plague?' Daddy can't sleep. When he can't sleep that's when he comes in my room.

Now she wakes in the loft, every ceiling fan spinning, the restless drone they make like locusts in the last days.

Where's Ross? she thinks, studying the big waterbed. *He was right here when I fell asleep.*

Throwing aside the blanket and getting to her naked feet, she tiptoes towards the kitchen to get a drink of water. Wait. What's that? She stops and rubs her sleepy eyes and stares dumbfounded at the thing that stands before her. It's shaped like a person. An empty milk gallon for a head. Thin metal and melted plastic fused and manipulated, everything bent and skewed towards one deliberate end; to conjure this figure, to bring it to life.

'Ross?' she calls, the hesitation in her voice a new thing. She turns and looks to the bathroom door. It's wide open. No water running. 'Ross, are you in there?'

No answer. The ceiling fans whir. The numbers on the digital clock by the bed are green. So is this girl come chasing fame. Turning back to the figure born overnight, she eyes its construction, its tortured posture, its parts.

Hmm, that's weird, she muses. *Where have I seen all this stuff before?*

Then it clicks. These are the steel shelves and hard plastic trays that belong to the refrigerator, the innards of the big icebox humming there against the wall.

Tracy looks around the loft one more time for her host. Then she heads for the fridge, skirting around the warped sculpture leaning in her path with a quick and athletic hop as if she fears the thing might somehow reach out and grab her.

When she opens the refrigerator door she's met with a bitter steam. And what she finds inside nearly makes her collapse, a hot wave through her brain, a sickness in her gut.

'What are you doing in there?' she says, her voice shaky. 'Why are you in there, Ross?'

And for the rest of her life she'll not forget the naked man's voice, nor his fetal pose, nor the look on his bluish face as it turned to address her, the rest of him Polaroid-still.

'Mom? A fire's coming. It starts in the forest. There's a God for these things. Didn't you know that? I know because I've seen his hooves. And how nimbly he steps. I used to choose the things he'd dance to. I used to say who'll sing and who'll not sing. But never mind that. How are you? Why were you gone so long? It's okay. I'm just happy you're here. Shhhhh. No time to waste. A forest fire is blind. And like all blind things it thrashes at the world. Firemen. Helicopters. I watch it eat them alive. Watch it spill into the freeway. Crackle in the dry trees. It eats through a skyscraper. It blows though a baby carriage. I can't know how it starts. Only that it's headed this way. And I burn. And I crackle and piss. I built a decoy while you slept. Quiet as a mouse. And came in here to hide where it's cool. Maybe I'll be okay here. If you really love me you'll close the door.'

Down in the street her eyes hunt for any kind of sign that will lead her to a bus stop, bus station. Halfway across Rose Avenue she hears Bebop's recorder blowing, faint at first but closer as she goes. A tune to get girls out of boxes. A tune to lure out every rat.

When she spies him swaying down by the coffee shop, the blue recorder to his lips, the tie-dyed turban towering atop his head, a faint smile graces her mouth. Craning her neck, Tracy lifts a hand and waves goodbye to the junky like a country-bound orphan might a new city friend. She doesn't wait for him to wave back. Just turns away and keeps walking, fast as her lily-white legs will go.

Down on Rose a bald kid lights a cigarette with a match. Further on two seagulls fight over half a burger on the pavement and a woman weeps into a cell phone, her make-up running down between the corners of her mouth. And in rolls the sea. Out rolls the sea.

GAY PARIS, NY

All through the night it rained. A fitful and violent downpour that kept Gloria drifting in and out of sleep, huddled in her unplugged electric blanket on the couch. The kind of rain that makes you feel lucky to have a roof over your head, and four walls, where the strange kinetic dervish of water and wind outside can't get you, can't hurt you.

Then she hears a crash and turns her head from its hiding place in a crease between the cushions. Peering out the window she sees the hard rain still slanting down, and the big blue tarp that shelters the flea market blowing awry in the grey light before sunrise.

Now she hears shuffling and muted curses from the back room. Emerging from their walk-in cooler turned honeymoon suite, Debbie and Joe go rushing though this cluttered main room and out the Dairy Queen's front door like a pair of paramedics into a shopping mall after an earthquake.

'Jesus Christ, not the porno playing cards I just scored!' Gloria hears Deb shout. 'Quick, grab 'em, Joe, they're from the fifties!'

Then she hears another sound. A different sound. It comes from upstairs. Lionel in his garret. Breathing in, she gets up from the couch and pulls her boots on and walks over to the ladder that leads to him and listens.

'I'm sorry I'm sorry I'm sorry I'm sorry,' is what it sounds like he's saying. Over and over.

'Lionel?' she says softly up the ladder. 'Are you okay?'

She listens for a response but nothing comes. Just the creepy broken record above. 'I'm sorry I'm sorry I'm sorry.'

Climbing up the ladder, her leg throbbing, Gloria thinks, *He must be dreaming.* And when she reaches the top and finds her bearings in this strange little room she stands here looking down at him in his narrow bed and knows it's not a good dream.

'I'm sorry I'm sorry I'm sorry I didn't stop them,' mutters the boy, his pale temple wet on the pillow, the sunglasses pinned to his face like a bad joke, Babar kicked to the floor.

'Black Jesus,' she says, lightly touching his foot. 'Wake up, it's just a dream.' When he doesn't stir she shakes him by the leg. 'Rise and shine, soldier!'

At this he springs up in his bed like a vampire in a B-movie, wrapping his hands around his chest as if it was freezing weather he woke to.

'Who are you?' he asks, his voice remote, brittle.

'It's me. Gloria. You're safe now. It's only a dream.'

'No it's not,' he says and something about the way he says it makes the dancer cold inside. 'Where's my mom?' he says.

'She's outside with Joe. The wind blew the tarp off its poles, things are blowing away.'

'I need my pills.'

Gloria doesn't answer.

'Can you get them for me?' says the boy.

'Are you sure you wanna keep taking those things? They can't be any good for you.'

'What else do I have?'

The stripper doesn't really know how to answer that.

'Please, Gloria.'

'Where are they?'

'Mom keeps 'em by the sink.'

On her way back up the ladder, the pill bottle in her back pocket, climbing with one hand, a glass of

water in the other, Gloria hears Bea Two-Feathers'
voice in her head: *A fence to keep in the sadness.*

So many different kinds of fences, thinks the
runaway as she clears the ladder's last rung. *White
picket. Electric. Barbed wire. Strip pole. Desert
camo. Pain meds. Old folks' home. What the fuck's
the difference?*

Now they sit side by side on Lionel's bed. In
her absence the boy must have reached down and
fished around on the floor for Babar because the
stuffed elephant joins them now in a tangle of
polyester blankets and bed sheets, his droopy gold
crown, his white tusks turned a deep grimy yellow
with time.

Contrary to the voice in her head, Gloria twists
off the hard top and taps out two big pale tablets
from the oversized flesh-colored bottle in her hand
boasting words like 'OxyContin', '60 MG', 'Keep
Out of Reach of Children'.

Then she puts them in his open palm. And he
pops them in his mouth. Now she lifts the cool
water to his lips and he drinks it down.

Outside in the blowing downpour they hear
Debbie yell, 'Hoist it, Joe! Hoist it!' Fat Deb, the
batty Ahab of Gay Paris.

'Thank you, Gloria.'

'For what? Feeding you this crap?'

'I don't know what else to do,' he says and his voice shakes, his hand shakes.

'I don't either,' she says and takes his cold hand. 'But I'm gonna help you find it.'

'I doubt it.'

'Really. I promise. Enjoy the high while you can. I think I know a way we can put these things to better use.'

VENICE BEACH, CA

When the refrigerator door swings open in the charged silence of this apartment, Ross Klein emerges alien, discolored, wide-eyed and gasping for air like a rescued Han Solo in the Hollywood space epoch of old.

A few blocks west you can hear Bebop's sad recorder blowing, soft but magnetic in its way. A melody to rock you, to heal you, to bless your life, to curse your fortune and blow you away. A little something to set you on your feet again, to lighten your load, to trick you into thinking that maybe you know what love means. A song to dazzle. One to spark a forest fire.

Standing here naked in his big vacant flat the critic catches his breath and has a last look around. The black sofa, the empty bed. The gleaming baseball bat in the corner. The silent record collection built into the wall. His German headphones. The bathroom door wide open, the dark mirror therein, the sink dripping slow, counting its own eerie time. And the drawn window shades at the far end of the space, a thin crack of light through the one Tracy was known to stand at singing songs she wrote that no one hears.

Now he turns back to the sculpture he built while she slept. The figure. Its milk-carton head leaning coy and childlike atop its bent shoulders. Its lunchmeat-drawer hips cocked in a way that might suggest the thing was hungry to strike up a jig. Its egg-rack feet at the ready. Its thin steel arms reaching.

Reaching for what?

Maybe for the thing we're all reaching for. That big feeling. The one we can't put our finger on, can't say its name.

Joy.

Love.

A clean conscience.

A cure for emptiness.

A warm putty to fill in all the holes that gape.

These things might approach it. But we reach for more. It's got to be out there. It just has to be.

Free nights and weekends.

Diet pill.

Radical cleric.

Get rid of worry lines.

Improvised explosive device.

Bible camp.

Blind carbon copy.

Who is this figure in the kitchen?

Maybe it's Ross as a boy, just about the time his mom disappeared. Or the poet he ached to be, frozen in distance and time somehow, still trying to find a song so fine it might whisper her home again.

Maybe it's some kid whose heart he broke with a bad review. Or maybe it's Gloria, or Desiree, or whatever the hell the stripper's real name is, dancing in the red sun, her fine legs back the way they were, bending to her pirouette at last: listen to the crowd. Or maybe the figure is you. Maybe it's me.

Now Ross does a strange thing. As gingerly as a schoolgirl on her last morning of classes, he walks over to the big bed, squats down and pulls out the black shoebox wherein Gloria's worn ballet slippers hide. Then he takes them out and forces them on one after the other and walks to the door and, finding the bolt already free, turns the knob and leaves for the street below.

These are days without limits. When a child can lie awake in its bed anywhere in suburbia with curiosity gnawing and climb from the blankets and enter the right search in the dark and sit watching a real man get his head hacked off with a long knife on the haunted screen, the shaky camerawork, the calm, bearded witnesses in the background, their alien headdress, different hats, different routes to heaven.

What color is God?

Does he have a videophone?

There are lovers on the windy beach of Venice, California. There are hustlers, find them where they perch. There is a man with a cotton candy machine. And one who sells cheap sunglasses. And the lady giving fortunes out for money. Where is it all headed? How does it play out?

Unshaven and pale of skin, Ross Klein comes reeling and foul down Rose Avenue in his white slippers, naked as the day he was born. It's a busy Saturday afternoon. A thousand tourists watch him come, like something they've seen before, some vision from the Prophecy Channel late at night. They pull their children close. They part the way to let him pass. *Who is this cracked nudist come among us? Why am I nauseous? Why am I thrilled?*

Then slowly, as if by some living contagion, these suntanned witnesses in colored shorts and flip-flops begin, one after another, to lift their cell phones and shoot. Lift your digital and shoot. Call the cops. Lift your disposable and shoot shoot shoot. Save this picture. Post it where you like. Share it with friends. Share your video. Post it for all to see.

It's not till he's halfway to the boardwalk that he really takes notice of the leering throng of low paparazzi gathered in rows on either side of his advance. Now he hears the clicking of their gear, senses the depth of their excitement, the high they feel, the puzzlement, their palpable righteousness and disgust. This fallen commenter come at last to be judged. Now who can count the limits of his shame?

He makes for the sea. The wind blows his hair. Gulls circle off above the pagodas. Something dead in the sand. Sun falling red. In his frightened gallop he collides with a girl on rollerskates just before he reaches the boardwalk, the headphones jerking from her ears like a net being snipped as she crashes to the asphalt. But look, like some demented hurdler Ross recovers, gains his footing, keeps on towards the crashing blue Pacific that beckons.

When he gets to the end of the pier he stops, out of breath, his hands on his knees, his head bent down. Then he stands up and looks at the water, his chest still heaving, all the air inside him tinged with the sick reality of his heart. There's a soda bottle dancing in the surf. And a plastic bag like a duped soul, jerked this way and that. Junky piper on the beach. Gulls. Sirens in the distance. Every helicopter scanning for fires. Every rat to the sea.

GAY PARIS, NY

'Where's Gloria?' says Black Jesus.

'Not sure, honey. She took off on her scooter a while ago, think she mighta said somethin' 'bout going to the store, though I can't imagine what she might need out there that she couldn't find right here at the DQ,' muses Debbie White and gives a proud glance about the flea market, scanning the whole of her worthless kingdom with a faint gleam in her eye that might be the beginnings of a tear. It's a warm day for October, geese in the sky from time to time, bright leaves on the ground, red, yellow, copper.

'Well, speak of the devil, here she is now,' says Deb turning to the gravel parking lot where the girl rumbles in and turns off her engine, kicks out the kickstand, yanks off her crazy helmet, the pink shield catching the sunlight as she hangs it on the handlebar.

'I'm still not a hundred per cent about this one yet, Lionel. Half the time it's like she's in some kind of dream world.'

'Look who's talkin', Ma.'

'Shhhhh,' whispers Deb. 'Here she comes.'

'Hi guys.'

'Hi Gloria, beautiful day, huh?'

'You can say that again.'

'Beautiful day,' says Black Jesus, twenty-four hours without his pills.

'How's business been?' says Gloria.

'Not too shabby. We sold the wolf painting. The big one that used to hang right there. About god-damn time. Got sixteen bucks for it.'

'It used to be on the wall in my room when I was a kid,' says Lionel. 'Then I swapped it for Iron Maiden, Stranger in a Strange Land.'

'What you got there, sweetie?' asks Deb, tossing her chin at the plastic grocery bag in Gloria's hand.

'Oh, just some stuff to make an angel food cake. Which brings me to my next question: Hey Debbie, do you mind if I use the kitchen?'

'Um, I'm not really sure I should just be letting anybody fire up that big—'

'Mom,' growls Lionel. 'Be easy for once in your life.'

'Okay, fine. You can bake your cake,' says Deb, a hot fist clenched in her sweatpants pocket. 'Just make sure you clean up after yourself.'

'No troubles, bubbles,' says Gloria with a smile on her face. 'Thanks a million.'

An hour later Gloria slides the wet batter in a deep silver pan into the oven at 350 degrees Fahrenheit and shuts the oven door and gets to work on the icing. Traditionally speaking, an angel food cake is served without any kind of glaze on top. But this cake isn't for just anyone.

Into a small pot on the cracked Formica counter she pours what she imagines to be half a cup of milk. Then with a match she lights a burner on the big industrial stove and picks up the pot and puts it on the flame. From her grocery bag she pulls a package of Price Chopper brand confectionery sugar and opens it with her teeth and pours half of it down into the simmering milk. Now she adds a little orange juice from the fridge and stirs the potion with an old noisy whisk she found in one of the grubby kitchen drawers at her waist.

Once it starts to thicken she lowers the heat and walks back towards the front of the Dairy Queen where the couch she sleeps on lies musty and still upon the old linoleum. Straddling the arm of the couch, she bends and lifts the plaid cushion beneath her electric blanket and fishes around and pulls out the bottle of OxyContin she commandeered from Lionel White, US Marine.

On her way back to the stove, she stops at a faded red milk crate on the floor in the helter-skelter of junk and boxes that dominate this once orderly summertime oasis and squats down and takes up the rusty hammer she's been eyeing all day, not ignoring the fact that even in this untested position her bad leg feels better than it has any time since that nightmare hour she left LA for good.

Back in the kitchen she stands and spreads a New York Post on the countertop. *Top military analysts say the troop surge is working . . . The dismembered body of a prostitute was discovered in a shopping bag outside the Galleria Mall in Poughkeepsie, this marks the third such incident this year . . . Michael Jackson's death linked to painkillers, doctor brought in for questioning. King of Pop or Wacko Jacko? Join our online poll.*

Gloria twists open the pill bottle and drains its contents onto the newspaper. Over a dozen fat white tablets in all. Tossing the bottle in the garbage, she squares her hips and sets to folding the New York Post over the drugs in a tight and careful manner, as one might go about shaping a child's paper boat for deployment in a bathtub.

Once the folds are secure, the girl reaches for the hammer and lifts it over her head and begins violently beating the newspaper, the noise of her bludgeon drowning out the simmering milk and sugar on the stove. Lucky for her, Debbie is two minutes away from selling a VCR to a Mexican couple out under the tarps or else she'd come running in to see what the racket was.

Setting the hammer aside and peeling back the edges of the paper, Gloria finds what she'd imagined: a fine powder lying white and halfway mystic upon the printed words, enough to knock out a horse.

So she turns to the stove and switches off the burner and folds the newspaper in half and dumps the powder down into the hot icing and whisks the pot until the two things are one.

She sets out for Serenity Grove on foot, the dancer we call Gloria. Before leaving the Dairy Queen she surprised Debbie by asking if it was okay for her to borrow some things to wear from the few tired clothing racks heaped with freakish miscellany scattered about the junk sale. A long fur coat, fake rabbit. A feathered bowler for her head. A battered pair of black stiletto boots. A blood-red teddy. Then she surprised Debbie and Lionel alike when she said,

'Meet me at Serenity Grove in an hour and fifteen. Six thirty sharp. Please don't argue with me. Bring Joe, he'll understand. Have the station wagon ready. Movie starts at seven!'

She walks the highway, the angel food cake in a wide hatbox held out before her in both hands like an offering, the garish outfit she chose inspiring more than one passionate honk, more than just a 'How much?' from the smokers in Shakespeare's gravel lot.

The lady at the front desk of this ridiculous eroding rural nursing home nearly faints into her cream of mushroom soup when Gloria breezes through the door and shimmies up to her and says, 'Singing telegram for Director Steve.'

Still in shock, the queasy secretary leads her down the tan hall and leaves her at a door that bears the man's name and title in gold decals. After adjusting her fur coat and smearing more lipstick on her red mouth, she knocks and hears him bark a muted, 'Just one minute,' paranoia in his voice as if the man might be finishing up some secret mischief of his own.

When he gets to the door with a jangling of keys and opens it and stands facing this callgirl in all her sleazy feline glory the first thing he thinks is, *Man alive, those Visualize Your Own Reality books on tape must be starting to work.*

'Do come in,' says the director, and as she brushes past him with the cake box in her hands he pops his balding head out into the hall to make sure the coast is clear, and seeing that indeed it is he shuts his office door again and locks it from the inside.

'To what do I owe this pleasure?' he says and sits down and leans back in his black swivel chair, fingers laced in his lap. The paneling on the walls looks like wood but of course it's not. It might be that this man has spent so many stale hours here that he's taken on the same diminished look as the shag carpet at his feet, the big telephone on the desk, the kinky paperweight, the grim roll of flypaper dangling from the ceiling. All his diplomas are perfectly straight where they hang. His audio books are all in a row. This is a very neat man. Everything in its right place. Then why does it feel so wrong?

Our heroine wastes no time. Deftly she sheds the fake rabbit and lets it fall to the floor in a heap to unveil the scant lingerie she chose, the skin beyond, the dark haunted patch below her pale belly.

'You must have done something really magnanimous in a past life,' she purrs, praying magnanimous was the right word to use.

'I don't doubt it,' admits Director Steve, his eyes wide.

'I think we need a little privacy,' she whispers. 'Why don't you send the staff on an errand for a few hours?'

'Touché. Great idea,' he whispers back, hard in his JC Penney business slacks. Picking up the phone on his desk he dials zero and waits for a voice and says, 'Janet? No I'm fine, she's an old friend of my sister. I was calling 'cause after seeing my friend here all dressed up like this I remembered Halloween is coming right up. Why don't you and Julio and Keith take the van down to Wal-Mart and pick out some costumes for yourselves and for the oldies but goodies in our charge. What? I don't care, you can be anything you want. No, it's okay, you can use the church donation box. No, don't worry, I've cleared it with the pastor.'

So let it be done. Not one of his underpaid peons will argue with that. All three of them abandon their posts and make for the Wal-Mart, ten miles east, where all things are found.

'*I think we're alone now,*' sings Gloria, and climbs on his lap and straddles the chair. '*There doesn't seem to be anyone around.*'

'*I think we're alone now,*' sings back the director in a shockingly pleasant alto. '*The beating of our hearts is the only sound.*'

Now the callgirl bends and reaches her hand down into the top of her tall boot and pulls out two thin candles and a plastic lighter. The 99-cent affair she stole in a different life, under a different sun, different name, when there where two kinds of deserts, the one she rode through, the one inside.

At least now she's got a use for it.

'Turn the lights out,' she demands.

'Lucky thing I've got the clapper,' he boasts and slaps his palms together twice and the room goes black. She can smell him. Their bodies this close. 'Lucky it's the clapper I've got,' he adds. 'And not the clap.' And his laugh in the dark is like a dead cat in a bag.

Sparking the lighter, she looks around in the soft glow and takes the cake from the box and sets it between them and plants the candles in the top and lights them both.

'One for beauty, one for the beast. Now open sesame,' says the stripper to the creep, and parting his mouth like a nurse might a fluey child's she stuffs his face full of angel food. He chews and slobbers and grabs at her tits and she jerks back and raises a finger and warns, 'No, no, no. Not till you've finished your treat. Then you can have your cake and eat me too.'

Once she's gotten all the icing down his throat she eases up off his crumby lap and climbs onto the desk.

And dances in the wavering light.

Then off with her hat.
And each sharp boot in turn.
Her crimson teddy to the floor like a soul falling.
Wet mouth.
Slow zipper.
Just like riding a bike.
Till the room starts to spin.
Till all movements lose their meaning.
And hanging by a string above, the flypaper turns immeasurably slow in the dark.

Bea stares out her open window, smoking one of her famous cigarettes, an elbow perched on the brown sill, a withered breast bent out of shape inside her nightgown. The setting sun throws a faint rosy haze on the lawn, and up among the branches of the dogwood tree, and past it, there where the woods meet the sky.

Wow, the days are getting shorter, thinks the prisoner. *And mine are numbered. Are you finishing your crosswords? Are you snipping the good coupons? Are you afraid to die? Don't let it get to you. Don't let it bring you down. Maybe death is just a new dress.*

Then a knock at the door. But today Bea Two-Feathers is in no rush to answer it. She smokes and watches the fine sunlight where it plays, birds in the fall air. Then she turns from the window and looks at the door. Another few quick knocks in a row, louder this time. The days of hiding her butts and spraying the peach aerosol can are done. How much more trouble can she get into? Walking across the tiny room with the cigarette burned low between her fingers, Bea twists the knob to find whoever she will.

'Oh good, it's you. I thought it mighta been that Nazi again.'

'I wouldn't worry about him,' says Gloria, breathing heavy from her run up the stairs, the bad air in the hall, the whole seedy escapade unfolding.

'I hoped you might come back. But what are you doing all done up like a floozy? Is it Halloween already? You know I used to have that same hat.'

'Bea?'

'What?'

'I've come to break you out.'

Hearing this the old woman smiles and slowly nods her head and pulls a final hit off her smoke and blows it out and says, 'Just like Papillon.'

'Bea?' says Gloria, standing here in her big white coat and heels.

'Yes, angel?'

'We really gotta go.'

'I get it. Just let me doll myself up a bit. It's not every day of your life you get sprung.'

'Okay, just hurry up.'

'I knew it the first time I laid eyes on you,' says Bea, rummaging through her dresser drawer now, tossing a yellow blouse over her shoulder and onto the floor, hunting deeper. 'When you left holding that poor soldier's hand I said to myself, that girl is something special.'

Deb's tan Chrysler wagon is idling at the big glass doors in front when Gloria pushes her way through them holding Bea by the arm. Falling leaves. Last light of day. The old woman's face shows a wonderful calm, her white hair blown by the wind.

Wide-eyed in the passenger seat with the window rolled down, Joe the Deputy smiles, his eyes moist, hard to believe what he's seeing.

'Gloria! How in God's name did you manage to—'

'No time to explain,' she pants, climbing with her fugitive into the back seat where Lionel waits in a hooded sweatshirt, his black glasses clinging, joy on his mouth at the sound of her voice. 'Debbie, get us the fuck out of here before all hell breaks loose.'

Twilight on the narrow mountain road. Geese in a pink sky. Green metal sign that reads 'Town of Hunter'. Tall pines. Steel-deck bridge across the winding creek. Another sign that warns 'Landslide Zone, Next ½ Mile'.

'Let's turn on the radio,' says Gloria.

'You don't have to twist my arm,' says Debbie White as she twists the knob. 'Phil Collins!' She declares and begins to sing, one hand on the steering-wheel, one on Joe's thigh, '*I can feel it coming in the air tonight.*'

Joe Two-Feathers can't help but join in, and Gloria too, even Bea knows the words, and now a whispery Lionel to everyone's delight, their voices like a broken prayer in the laboring Chrysler. '*I've been waiting for this moment for all my life.*'

When they pull up to the shabby little ticket booth the old man inside seems surprised to see a car full of paying customers. With a head like a potato and kind blue eyes, in a voice that shakes because the sun's gone down and his heater's broke, he says, 'Evening, moviegoers. It's six fifty a head. Buy four, get one free. End of the season special. That makes it twenty-seven fifty.'

Nobody in the station wagon can find it in their heart to argue with his dubious math, or the fact that one of their number can't see; not even Deb. Joe opens his wallet and leans over his big breathing love and reaches out the window and hands the old timer a twenty and a ten and tells him keep the change.

'Thanks,' says the man in the booth. 'Tune your radio to 88.9 FM and enjoy the show. All we ask is no booze and no sex.'

'Sure thing,' says Deb and knocks the transmission back in drive and pulls ahead into the wide barren lot, thin weeds rising spectral in the headlights, snack bar off to the side, black Coke on ice, greasy popcorn, long red licorice, tall dark trees past the fence.

And in the open air before them looms the very thing they've journeyed past Hunter to behold. The drive-in movie screen. A titan in decay, pale and gaping, slashed and grainy when the projector starts to roll. This is a love story. And Bea will smile as it plays, and weep when it plays, the cancer just a ghost in her chest. And from time to time Gloria will lean and whisper in Lionel's ear so he might know how the story goes. And the wind blows the trees. And the heater rattles in the dash. But at least it warms the car. And we'll all sit together, our eyes on the giant screen in the dark, one of just three left in the state, sad relic of yesteryear, when everybody went to sleep at night still believing this was God's country.

PART
THREE

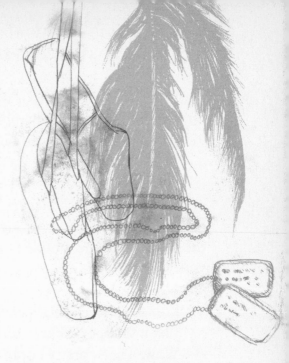

Because thin white birch trees stand naked down the path they walk. Because their pale branches grope for something beyond themselves. Because the sun just came up and the pastel glow it casts paints all things rare, their faces, the rusted-out truck they pass, the boots they wear, their fingers laced together, that vodka bottle in the leaves. Because November is a dying time. Because the pond she's led him to is so still. Because life is so strange, so real. Because we all got holes to fill. That's why we stick around.

Gloria sits down in the dewy leaves and cool grass by the water's edge, still gripping Lionel's hand, and helps the blind boy lower his body down here beside her. Tall cattails grow along the warped oval of the pond, their brick-brown heads like big dark corndogs swaying in a light wind. Faint woodsmoke on the wind, so good when it hits.

'A kid I knew drowned here.'

'Black Jesus?'

'What?'

'I'm not really a ballerina.'

He doesn't answer straight off, just listens to the quiet field, the woods at his back. 'So what are you?'

'Nothing.'

'I don't believe that.'

'Just a stripper,' she says. 'Used to be a stripper.'

'Wow. That's pretty cool.'

'It paid the bills. But I think I attracted the wrong people. That's what got me in a lot of trouble.'

'You danced on a pole?'

'Yeah.'

'And picked dollars up with your beaver?'

'Yeah. Even did handjobs in the Velvet Room. God it seems like a different world now.'

'Are you ashamed?'

'Not really. Just a little creeped out.'

'How did you keep on doing it?'

'I took a lot of showers,' she says, staring at the cold pond. 'I almost did an audition for a ballet company out there. But then I got hurt and ran away. And now here I am in Gay Paris, New York, falling for a soldier. Who woulda guessed.'

'What'd you say?'

'What part?'

'The soldier part.'

'Never mind.'

They sit in the silence they've made. Beech smoke like ghosts, streaming from a chimney.

'Something happened over there, Gloria,' he says, his cool rough hand in hers.

'I know. You got blown up. And now you're blind because of it. For the rest of your life you're blind. I can't even start to imagine how that feels. I've tried, but I can't.'

'That's not what I mean. It's not what happened to me. It's what I saw. Something I saw.'

Gloria breathes, treading lightly. 'The dancer I heard you talking about?'

Here the Marine gives out an ugly little laugh and says, 'Oh—that. No. I think the IED knocked my head so fuckin' bad I was just seeing things. Like some kind of guardian angel I wished was there for me.'

'Maybe that's what it was.'

'An angel?'

'Stranger things have happened,' says the dancer.

Black Jesus breathes in. Then he exhales, his breath a pale cloud in the chill morning air. 'Gloria?'

'What?'

'There's no angels in Iraq.'

Apart from the silence now they hear the sound of blowing leaves, distant cars down on 23A, a dog barking someplace.

'Maybe I just made her up to help me forget about what really went down,' says the boy. 'Then when you came around I think she turned into you, the dancer I mean, or you turned into her or whatever. I don't know. I was just so sad and busted, and the dreams wouldn't stop, and I wanted to look at everything I missed but I couldn't, and my head hurt, and all the pills. It got to be that hearing your voice or just you being around was the only thing that could keep my mind off it.'

'Off what?'

'I've been afraid to tell,' he says and lowers his head, his voice small and haunted. 'I didn't tell anybody.'

This is when she takes his hand and brings it in against her warm side. 'You can tell me.'

'I wasn't supposed to be there, Gloria,' he says, lifting his head to face her, the obscene glasses that hide his wounds, his wounds more real than ever. 'They were building a Burger King. It was a jobsite. Like a roped-off lot where they'd laid a slab and started nailing up the walls. It musta been Sunday or somethin' 'cause the place was empty. I was supposed to be helping keep watch at the checkpoint, but I had just seen a Marine, a guy I ate with

172

sometimes, they called him House of Blues 'cause he's big and plays harmonica, I'd just seen him get shot in the face the day before. The bullet blew the back of his head off, he was right next to me, as close as me and you, we never even saw where the shot came from, then his brains were on my hands, all over my pants, so I was shook up the next day. I told the squad leader I was going to piss and I took off and found the Burger King and hid there with my back against the wall like a big pussy.'

'You were scared,' she says, knowing how cold his hand feels in hers.

'Like a little girl,' he says, a wind blowing over the field where they lay, rippling the water, blowing his pale hair, rattling the dead cattails. 'I hid there a long time. From where I was I could see a sign the builders musta stuck in the ground. I don't know why but I kept on reading it. Over and over. 'Liberty Corp: Working hand in hand with your community to build a brighter tomorrow.' After a while I fell asleep. Then I heard the truck.'

Quiet in the field. Gloria's heart. Barking dog far away.

'It was one of ours. A Humvee. I watched it pull into the lot. First I thought they were lookin' for me, so I was shittin' my pants, keepin' real still. But when they got out I saw they had a girl in the back. A hadji. They pulled her out by her hair and threw her on the ground. I knew these guys. Three of them. Drunk as skunks. I could tell by the way they talked to her they thought she was hidin' somebody, a sniper prob'ly, prob'ly the hadji fucker who got House of Blues. So I guess they figured she had it comin' to her. And man did they give it. I watched 'em give it. Like a pack of dogs. Couldn't look away,' says Black Jesus. 'Couldn't even look away.'

Gloria watches his mouth as he talks. Any boyishness or innocence she might have marveled at there these past months is gone. Nowhere in sight. The thin dry lips like a whitewashed tire somebody left in the sun after the car it belonged to killed a kid in a hit-and-run somewhere in the American desert.

'Then everything happened so quick. They were done with her and they picked her up and two of 'em held her against the Burger King wall while the other one picked up a nail gun somebody left and nailed her hands to the wood. She didn't even cry, just hung there with her arms out and stared at them. One of 'em went to the Humvee and came back with a gas can and soaked her up till she shined in the headlights. Then he lit a cigarette and smoked on it once and pitched it at her and it hit her hair and lit her up like a Christmas tree.'

'Oh no,' she says. 'Oh no. Come here,' she says and pulls him close, his head against her chest, her arms around him like a hypothermic child. Child who shakes. Child who knows exactly how to kill. Who was a very good shot in his time. Who's bottled up a billion tears in the black interim.

'It's okay to cry,' says Gloria, looking out at the pond. 'I won't tell anybody,' she says, and soon his tears are hot on her sweatshirt.

'I didn't help her,' he wheezes. 'Even after they left. She was screaming. And crackling. And I didn't help her.'

Cattails knock. And colored leaves spin down. And by some reflex Gloria moves and touches her lips to the back of his neck. 'You were afraid.'

He can smell her. The shampoo she used days ago, faint, hypnotic. Her nice sweat. Some kind of faded rose, tangerine. Then his mouth is on hers. His warm wet face. Then her palms are to his temples. And her spine is to the cool grass, her wild dark hair falling all around. Her hand up his shirt, his pounding ribcage hot to the touch.

'Take your glasses off.'

'No.'

'Can I?'

'If you really want.'

'Thank you.'

Black plastic falling to the earth. Her damp kiss on the bridge of his nose like a morphine shot. Her hand in his jeans. He cannot see the wilderness in her green eyes as they gleam and stare but he knows they are beautiful beyond all description. Then her lips again. Then the buckle on her belt. The warmth and smell of her belly. Tangerine. The sound of her tight pants rustling down in the dead leaves.

He did this once before. Drunk with a Chinese hooker near the base where he trained. But that's a dead world. Gloria's breath at his ear now, the delicate drum inside. Drum to go to war. Drum to shake the night away. Drum to dance down a rain so real it'll scour all this history.

Days without limit. Pale sinners in the painted leaves. Each of them nineteen years on this earth. Where anything can happen. Where cattails knock by a pond as still as glass.

'Your favorite disk jockey Mike London checking in with the midday weather summary. There's a low-pressure system moving through carrying cloudy skies for the whole Hudson River Valley and into the Southern Catskills. Eighty percent chance of rain this afternoon, skies clearing up around dark. Highs in the mid to low fifties. I tell you what, I've been suffering severe Eurythmics withdrawal ever since my wife's cat peed on every "E" in my CD library. I was just about to spin "Here Comes the Rain Again" but then I had second thoughts, didn't wanna jinx us. So here they

*are, Annie Lennox and that other guy, with their
1983 smash "Sweet Dreams".'*

'Turn it up!' yells Debbie in a wool hat with a
multicolored pom-pom on top. 'I love that crazy
redhead bitch.'

'Sure thing,' says Bea Two-Feathers, rocking
away in Lionel's old wicker chair, all bundled up in
a big puffy coat and scarf, a mittened hand already
on the boom box, jacking the volume.

*Sweet dreams are made of this, who am I to
disagree? Travel the world and the seven seas, everybody's lookin' for something.*

'I know what I'm lookin' for,' says Joe, grabbing
Deb by the waist and doing his best Patrick Swayze.
'I got everything I want right here in Gay Paris, right
here at the old DQ.' Now he spins the big woman
around. 'Woo-weee. Ain't that right, baby doll? One
man's junk is another's delight!'

'Shit, you better believe it, I already sold a ski
jacket and a dartboard and that lady who died's
exercise bike, all before noon! I'm so hot I'm swea-
tin' like a whore in church.'

'I second that emotion,' howls Joe the Deputy,
and a prefab modular home wrapped in plastic
strapped to a flatbed truck lumbers past on its way
to answer other dreams.

Now here come Lionel and Gloria right behind,
easing the battered moped into Dairy Queen's

parking lot with their helmets gleaming in the
cold sun.

'You two came home just in time,' yells a dancing Deb. 'Radio just said it's supposed to rain.' Then
she looks Joe in his dark Mohawk eyes and sings
along, '*Hold your head up, movin' on. Keep your
head up, movin' on.*'

'Hi kids,' says Bea with a mitten in the air.

'Hi Bea,' says Gloria, come among them.

'How you feelin', Bea?' says Black Jesus.

'Can't complain. I saw on the TV yesterday a
thing about a man who put a toaster oven in his
mother's bubble bath 'cause he couldn't afford her
medicine.'

'Don't be such a bummer, Ma,' yells Joe.

'How's your breathing?' asks Gloria.

'Just fine,' lies Bea. 'I feel like Raquel Welch. The
Big Medicine's on my side. It's gonna take more
than a doomsday verdict from some Albany quack
to get rid of me.' Then quietly to Gloria, 'You got
a light?'

'I heard that, Ma,' says Joe.

Glancing over at the tall cop, Gloria meets his
eyes and tilts her head and shrugs her shoulders and
fishes in her pocket and pulls out the Trade Center
Memorial lighter she stole in another world and
hands it lovingly to Bea.

'Thank you, dear,' says the old woman, holding

the soft pack of smokes in her mitten and shaking one loose into her mouth.

'Keep it,' says the stripper.

At Debbie's urging they took an umbrella from an old pickle barrel filled with such things for sale and crossed the highway and picked up the trail behind the stone church and followed it haltingly down to the creek. Stones underfoot, worn roots that lace the way, laid bare by time.

With the closed umbrella flung over her shoulder like some punk-rock Mary Poppins, Gloria stops and steps lightly up and helps her soldier onto the rotting planks of the Swinging Bridge.

Halfway across, his hand in hers, any danger tempered by the way they feel, he marvels, 'Listen to the water.'

The hard autumn rains have turned the Kaaterskill into a violent thing. Cool and clear in the summer months, it goes brick-red this time of year, kicking up earth as it twists down the mountain, brick-red as the faces of the half-naked race that fished its banks in the long ago, wild paint on cheek and brow, rough jewelry and furs, dance-fires waiting as night fell, songs to the rich earth, songs of birth and blood. All before the Marlboro Man drew his gun.

'That's the first time I heard it that way.'

'The Creek?' she says.

'Yeah, it's like music,' says the boy.

Dusk finds them on the edge of town. There's an abandoned nuns' camp here where, in the years between the world wars, troubled street kids from New York City would come spend their summers in these woods under the hard, loving eyes of the Gay Paris Sisters. Upon the wide sweep of camp ground a few ruins remain. The long screened-in cafeteria with its slab foundation and failing roof. The little bygone chapel/playhouse where they all would sing. The olde world pump house. The swings.

And here they swing, their charged legs working double time in the falling light, November's sun lost in the woods behind their backs to birth a rough pink seam where the mountain meets the sky.

'Weeeee-hoooo! I haven't done this since my balls were bald,' yells the Marine. 'Never felt this good.'

The rain did come, as prophesied by the DJ, but only a passing shower. On the long walk here they felt the first drops hit and Gloria popped open the umbrella and the two of them huddled beneath it as the rain came and went.

Now the wet ground smells alive. And the wind inhabits their faces and hair as they swing, the arcs they travel hanging kinetic in the dusk, mysterious even to them. The speed at which they move. The way their paths cross in the air. The loud wind. The rusty frame moaning under their weight. The chains that hold them creaking as daylight dies.

'Maybe I've always been blind.'

'What?' calls the girl as she swings into the future, craning her neck back to find him. 'I didn't hear you.'

'Maybe I've been blind all my life.'

Walking home along the highway in the dark, a few tired streetlamps to guide them, Gloria pulls Lionel White into the empty lot beside Shakespeare's Bar & Grill.

Cracked asphalt at their feet, pale dandelions. The moon a swollen penny overhead. Fresh world after the rain. Wet leaves. Wet hair. Wet road.

There are maps in the night sky that might help us know where we come from. And there are rotting maps in the glove box of Interstate's ancient rig that falls to ruin in the field behind the bar. Every known ribbon of highway therein. But will these highways lead us home? Roaming charge. Self-storage unit. Meth lab. New kind of war. We're slashing prices, all year-end stock must go! Identity theft. Tanning hut. Reality show. Toxic asset. Attention deficit hyperactivity disorder. There are six pharmacies on one street in the promised land. But is there balm in this land?

The stripper touches his face. 'Wanna dance?'

'No thanks,' he says.

'Why not?'

'I'd feel like a homo.'

Gloria laughs, her hot breath flying off into the cold air, her fingers letting fall the umbrella so she can reach for the small of his back, her belly to his.

Till they rock softly in the empty lot, his maimed cheek against hers, her palm on his sweatshirt, his young heart inside, a faint metronome to set the tempo of their lost waltz.

This is how they'll mend. This is how they'll dance the night away. Dance clean the darkness. Darkness inside, darkness out.

Till she hums. A song to patch the holes. The ones that gape. Ten miles to the east stands a Super Wal-Mart, biggest in the state, and it hums too, all day and night, weird and incessant. But they don't hear it. Not these kids. Not tonight. Not in Gay Paris. Where the red creek runs. Where a trailer lies burnt and rusting on its bank. Where cornfields stand withering and sere. Where a stoplight changes color forever and swings in the wind like a hanged witch. And a coke dealer taps his foot as he rigs his scale. And a boom box plays soft hits, yesterday's favorites.

What happened to the twentieth century? Where did it go? Is time just a plastic explosive? Did we splinter to the four winds? Are we doves when we close our eyes? Are we killers when we sleep? Do we frighten easy? Do we shake when the phone goes dead?

We who are each but a pixel, and horny for many things, and smaller than a stone on the beach, and just as beautiful, just as coarse.

What are we headed for? How does it all play out? Will something come and swallow us one still winter's day? Will we dance down a scary rain? A dollar-store pestilence? A blinding flash of light? A pale horse no soft hit can soothe? I can feel it coming in the air tonight. I've been waiting for this moment for all my life. I was there and I saw what you did. Saw it with my own two eyes.

ACKNOWLEDGEMENTS

Page	Song
4	'Islands in the Stream' Words and music by Barry Gibb, Maurice Gibb and Robin Gibb © Copyright 1983 Gibb Brothers Music (66.66%) Used by permission of Music Sales Limited. All Rights Reserved. International Copyright Secured.
76, 103	'We Will Rock You' Words and music by Brian May © 1977, Reproduced by permission of Queen Music Ltd/ EMI Music Publishing Ltd, London W8 5SW.
85–6	'Private Dancer' Words and music by Mark Knopfler © Copyright 1984 Straitjacket Songs Limited. Used by permission of Music Sales Limited. All Rights Reserved. International Copyright Secured.